CHEMICAL SAUSAGE

and other stories

J.J. Patrick

First published in the United Kingdom 20th July 2018 by

Chemical Sausage and other stories

First Edition

ISBN 978-1-9164086-0-9

My Ruby,

Without you, words are not love. See?

E-COMMERCE

That theer dingy bog a't' Blue Note reeked uh stale wazz un Southern Comfort but thon cubicles were miraculously clean. Folk Vommin' in't urinals un ower't' sticky, black dogshelf instead, leaving glowin' globs ayit int' UV light tuh avoid contaminatin' true heart uht' club – them flat, white ceramic cistern tops frum weer speed un coke were dabbed un snorted, once t'often wettin' wraps, sliced un cut frum magazines then artfully folded, 'ad been tecken frum kecks un pockets un socks un mingin' shoes.

Onl't' unlucky ones, back in them days, would find 'emselves 'awkin about wit' condensated dealy bags – them little plastic ziplock packets in which t' stodged gear would sweat un liquify. There wah no bangin' ont' doors, no disturbance frum t' bouncers. Both were ont' payroll, patiently ignorin' allt' drug use un only turning away't' types uh punters likely tuh disturb't' peace by gettin' bladdered, bein' bladdered, or wearing shoes which indicated thay'd not come tuh enjoy't' secret delights uh Aas Music un illicit, class A, chemical substances.

Int' dark club, painted blacker thun sky ower Bill's mother's, which would accommodate nuh more thun three-hun'red people at its wost fire risk, provision uh'a weekend 'aven at't' Friday Club wah crucial tuh its continued success as a tax free, money makin' vehicle weert' bulk uh legitimate sales come frum bottled water un dinky lollipops. Sat'day night saw its return tuht' drinkers, tuht' owder generation uh Derby's more tradishnul sloshin' culture, but Friday wah a day uh worship at t'alter uh thumping beats un uplifting vocals, weer DJs like that Jeremy Healey un Alistair Whitehead would be just as mashed as t' dancin' throng, whoopin' un blartin' theer hearts int' old disco style, un shaking euhporic sweaty 'ands at th'ends uh theer sets.

'Ad it not been furt' escape tuh Wilmorton's grubby inner-city college, away frumt' maddening snootery uht' wannabe grammar school int' village, Jack might never uv come tuh experience t' bitter taste uh anphetamines, t' nasal burn uh coke, ort' sheer joy uh a white dove. Ecstasy. A stomach-tinglin', man-made joy int' form uh a tiny stamped pill, cooked up in an Amsterdam lab un lovingly smuggled intuh his 'and at't' cost uh a ten pound palm cross tuh Winston. T' big, hamfisted lump made't' perfect stooge, uh course. Imbecillic un delighted tuh carry enough drugs un cash upon his person 'tween 'andovers tuht' club tuh send him far on wi' slops fur a very considerable period. He wah equally happy, tuh carry a lock knife, happen, in case things went wonky. Despite also bein't' only punter int' joint who wah allowed tuh hold ontuh a glass pint pot, in case a glassing wah required.

Poor owed Winstuhn di'n't really see what wah coming when Jack first spotted his own opportunity tuh make a dent ont' local economy – though it di'n't cross his mind until't' end uh that first three months as a recreational fuckhead, coz't' high wah new un obliterated everythin' but't' absolute enjoyment uh it. That tingling sensation int' chest or belly as't' glorious concoctions began tuh release 'emselves intuh't' body, that shimmer-shake int' major muscle groups as 'is blood pumped't' artificial stimulation tuht' limbs, then't' owerwhelming headrush as allt' brain's electrical impulses began tuh fire un't' world changed shape un tone under't' forced dilation uht' pupils – greedily takin' in light, even int' black uht' club.

Jack ad'n't been very good at cannabis, neither skunk nor resin had particularly grabbed him, un buckets un bongs had always led him tuh coughing fits, red eyes, un a slight nausea which disrupted his enthusiasm. He wah also an outdoor lad un theer wa'n't much worse than sitting in a aas, surrounded by a cloud uh thick un smoggy pipe smoke produced by a group uh five or six teenage boys, stale stench uh bongwater mixing with that unpleasant pong uh trainers. Even whent' drinking years had started, when he wah fourteen, Jack had never really taken tuh that either. 'E could shotgun a can uh lager witht' best uh 'um, un he could wipe aat a tenner's worth uh one pound pints at Berlins no bother, but alcohol, like t' weed, provided too many setbacks fur it tuh be fully enjoyed. Hangowers were a cripplin' ruination uht' day which followed t' night out un, when you took it a step too far in taan, theer wah always't' risk you'd end up spewing all ower yourself just as't' girl yud been watching all night met your peepers.

No, neither dope nor booze were a good fit fur young Jack but, 's'if tuh prove t'old parental fear about gateway drugs true, it wah both which provided Jack wit' access tuh a world in which he found himself as happy as a pig int' proverbial shit. It wah through college he met Matt and it wah through a night aat fur drinks wiy Matt that he finally became acquainted wit' delectible feast uh Derby's controlled substance underground uh 1996.

RUN

In that moment, when your life collapses around you, what can you do? One minute I was just out of the shower, warming up nicely after a winter's day planting trees, and next? Well, next I was sat on the sofa, a lump of mashed potato cooling down in my mouth, while my girlfriend of five years was busy telling me it was over and she had met somebody else.

So what can you do? Personally, I started by spitting out the mashed potato and binning the rest of it, still steaming. Then I packed her bags of *I'll just keep these here* belongings and, rather unceremoniously, showed her the door. Obviously, she did know where the door was but I was just making sure. Being thorough. She had said, while on the sofa, she couldn't see where we were going and that I didn't challenge her, not like the new man did. At least now she could see perfectly she was going outside and I was staying inside.

'Oh and if you want a challenge, try getting back in!' I shouted at her through the leaded door-glass, before turning my back and plodding into the kitchen, shoulders slumped.

Even as I walked away from her, as she in turn walked away from us – by which I mean me - she had to have the final word. 'I can't believe you're being like this. I'm totally honest with you and you act like a total cock! Good luck in life, you'll need it. LOSER!'

Rather than make myself the villain of the piece by shouting insults back, I softly closed the kitchen door and leaned with my forehead against it until I heard the gravelly crunch-stomping of her feet stop at the end of the driveway, followed by her car door slamming shut. I then shuffled slowly on my feet until my back was flat against the door. Staring up at the ceiling, as the noise of her car engine faded into silence, I realised I had been holding my breath and exhaled.

For the first time in a very long time I felt a quiver in the back of my throat as I stood there, breathing now but still staring up at nothing in particular. This soon developed into a full blown crying fit and I sank down to a sitting position, my back still against the door, buttocks planted firmly on the cold quarry tiles and knees drawn up to my chest. Call me a great big wet blanket, but I couldn't think of anything else to do except carry on. Nobody ever tells you what this part of being in a relationship is like - the bit where your 'other half' tap dances on the heart she's just pulled, still beating, from your chest. I could have smashed things up but decided smashing my own things up was not a good idea and stuck with crying.

When I'd finished with the out and out bawling, but was still sobbing, I found I still didn't know what to do. I did however find that all of the change had slid from my pockets onto the floor. I hadn't even noticed the clattering of coin on tile and absently picked up a fifty pence piece and began flipping it, catching it each time on the back of my palm. I wiped my eyes on my sleeve, absently flipped and caught the coin, and looked around the kitchen. The photograph caught my eye immediately. Blue sky, blue sea, white sand, friends, smiles, heat. I looked at the picture, then at the coin. Then back at the picture and the poster behind it. I had an idea for something else I could do.

I tossed the coin and quietly said the word *heads* into the otherwise quiet room. Heads it was.

So, when your life collapses around you what can you do? Well, to anyone who would care to listen I can safely say: let them have the last word. Then cry. Then toss a coin and stick to whatever it tells you to do.

***

Ow, ow, ow. OW! Opening eyes equals pain. Hardly $E=mc^2$, I know but, at this moment in time, it's just as true.

Swiftly I squeeze both eyes shut again and contemplate keeping them that way for the rest of my natural born life. However, the time has come. I must face my hangover, shower and go out for breakfast. It won't actually be breakfast though, probably *high-tea* is more appropriate. In fact, there won't be any tea either, so that leaves me pondering for a moment: *is it acceptable for a non-American to use the word high, in the sense of it referring to being drunk?* Meanwhile, having tricked my brain into thinking about something else, I open my eyes.

Once again I'm hit by a display of brightly coloured, eye-fireworks as the light of the room floods my vision. This causes me to groan and the imaginary man wielding the axe swings it once more, straight into my left temple. I lay there groaning some more but persevere at keeping my eyes open and, after about a minute, become quite good at it. Big, gold star for me.

The night before starts to come back to me in a patchwork of disjointed images. It's like watching Pulp Fiction for the first time, when you don't really know how it's all going to come together but it somehow all makes sense in the end. At first all I get is flashing lights, a nightclub, people everywhere dancing. Then a table pops in the mix too, at first it's empty but it gets gradually covered in empty drinks glasses. Every colour of the rainbow is in the bottom of them. I imagine a relapsed alcoholic Munchkin would drink much the same. I can even remember once piece of music which definitely played, a bouncy, old house track by Livin' Joy. I've got it somewhere on a mix CD but, with my headache as it is, now is not the time to turn on, tune in and drop out. Turn on, tune in and drop dead would be more likely, as my brain feels like it actually may explode. And I'm still haunted by that scene from Scanners.

Eventually my image of the night is complete and, to sum up, I was drunk and it was fun. Feeling like a really brave little soldier I sit up slowly and immediately have to hold both hands to my head, to stop my skull cracking at each side as my grey matter tries to flee in search of a safer home. I resume groaning and finish off the sitting up process very slowly.

Another couple of minutes pass and I'm still feeling brave and even a little bit adventurous. I also need use the toilet before I do something I haven't since I was a very young child. Attractive I know, but I'm only talking about piss. I had a friend once who repeatedly shit the bed when drunk. He never stayed over at my house. Knowing my options are limited I slowly swing myself sideways and lower my feet out of the bed, through the air, and down to the cool floor tiles. It feels wonderful and I almost want to get all of my twenty-six-year-old self down there to press my head against the same ceramic.

The sun only enters the room in strips of light due to the shutters and, as I inch my feet forward to a new cool patch, the light hits my toes. Even in the small quantity of solar energy from one of these shuttered out strips I can feel the heat from outside and I'm glad my apartment is air conditioned.

My blood flow adjusts nicely to this new sitting position and, mercifully, as some of the pressure is relieved from my head, the headache starts to feel a little better. Then, disaster. As I purvey the strewn mess of clothes across my floor, dropped where I left them earlier in the day, my foot catches an empty wine bottle near to the bed. It rolls across the tiled floor making the most horrendous noise. In my head it's amplified. First the hollow sounding *cu-cruin-cu-cruin-cu-cruin* noise of the bottle, as it makes it's full turns - tile to grout line. Along with that a constant, underlying *screeeeeeeeee* sound, made by the tile against glass. My head hurts more again and it seems someone has turned the volume up on my house, just to spite me.

I lose yet more time after this horrific noise deluge, sitting on the edge of the bed with my face buried in my hands, moaning softly. Occasionally I whimper too, just for good measure. Then the time comes. A man must do what a man must do. Bite the bullet. Take the bull by the horns. Get out of bed and walk to the bathroom.

***

Finally I hit the main square and the bar is straight ahead. The cool shade of the overhanging vines on the pergola looks very inviting. Suddenly, I feel like someone who has been crawling around in the desert looking for water.

The afternoon has been hotter than a day in Hell's pancake factory and I can feel the ground baking the soles of my open, Summer shoes. I'm also sweating faintly and I can just about smell last night's alcoholic beverages seeping out through my pores. I decide very quickly I am an actual, real live tramp. I am also, officially, in phase three of my hangover, with headache and nausea having already passed. Not long now and I'll be in phase four, recovery, swiftly followed by more punishment.

The bar is quiet at this time of day and I walk into the bliss of the shady terrace and plonk myself into a chrome chair. Right by the street, I have a perfect view of any passing human traffic which might catch my attention - my attention having already been caught several times by the freshly arrived tourists on the five minute walk from my apartment building. God I love this place.

I see a waiter doing the rounds inside. It looks very dark in the vaulted inner bar by comparison to the shaded terrace and I'm not sure he'll see me but then, recognition.

His hand goes up and he indicates he'll be with me shortly. I nod and smile then sit back. The chair creaks. I will always get, either a creaky chair or wonky table, it's a family tradition. Failing that something will break, I will walk into a lamp-post or someone will punch me. It's the law.

I take a bit more interest in the three men sat a couple of tables away. The one in the middle seems to be holding court and is quite animated, moving his hands a lot and the blue smoke which drifts up from the end of his cigarette makes some very interesting swirls and hoops in the perfectly still air. I catch the faintest scent of it and it smells nice. I stopped smoking a couple of months ago but the aroma of a cigarette, when it's at least six feet away, is still quite pleasant. It reminds me of a far, far away, once upon a time part of my early teenage years. In those endless summer days, when school was out and nothing else was in, I used to hang around with a lad called Dan and we used to steal pale beige packets of Camel from his parents. I mean, they had kitchen cupboards full of them, what were we supposed to do? Anyway, we used to take them down the disused railway track and stash them under the sleepers, halfway down the old, smoke-blackened tunnel. Christ we'd spend hours down there, setting off bangers under bottles and cans, firing air pistols, BB Guns, throwing knives. Boys stuff. Of course we smoked too, but those packets of twenty would last a week or more. To start with. By the September I was addicted. I guess that's how it happens - on the park, on the railway, on the street, hanging around by the shops. Some kids do it and stop, some kids never do it. Some kids carry on, even if it's bad for them.

I was one of the latter and now, sitting at the bar, faint smell of six-feet, safe-distance cigarette smoke hanging in the still air, the railway track seems both far away and very close. It's a funny sensation, like a déjà vu but not quite full blown. I revel in quirky little natural highs like this, one of life's surprise perks.

The leader of the pack on the table of three is still gesturing frantically and the trio laugh in unison, unaware of the unexpected kick they've just injected into my afternoon. I lean forward a little to see if I can listen in and find out what's so funny but, just as I do, the waiter steps out of the gloom in my peripheral vision and comes straight to me. He smiles in recognition - I've been here everyday this week - but we're not on first name terms.

'Buono Pomeriggio, cosa ti porto?' he asks and I look up, as if thinking about what I do want. I'm not actually thinking about that at all, I've just seen a wasp the size of my index finger fly over the top of his shoulder, up into the foliage of the vines. I hate wasps. Wasps scare me almost as much as clowns. I mean, what the fuck are they all about? In fact what the fuck are wasps about while I'm asking?

'Latte macchiato ed un doppio vermentino, per favore.' I reply, only once I'm satisfied the wasp isn't going to dive bomb me. A café latte and a large dry, white wine - a Vermentino - is the order of the day for me.

The waiter looks unconvinced and asks me 'Sei sicuro?'

To re-assure him I am indeed sure, I smile and nod my head before saying 'Molto!' - very - to underline my point.

He shakes his head at my frankly disturbing combination of hot milk and booze but accepts I am the customer and therefore must be right. 'Arriva subito,' he finishes and with a further shake of his head walks back into the gloom. *Be right back.*

I take the opportunity to check my phone and, after some fidgeting, eventually manage to fish it out of my pocket. No calls or messages yet. The three men burst into laughter again and chink their beer glasses together. I get now they are telling jokes, hence the long dialogues and frantic gesturing followed by raucous bursts of laughter. I remind myself to listen in - I might pick up a joke or two to use later – and, with that, the waiter is right back just as promised. He sets down a coffee and a large white wine in front of me. The wine is almost freezing, which is good, it'll keep cool for a while. Vermentino is a nice, crisp wine and it doesn't go straight to your head. I've been drinking bucket loads of it. In fact, it's my main source of liquid. Which cannot be good. Surely. However, it is much better than wasps or clowns. 'Grazie mille,' I say to the now hovering waiter, then take the hint and ask how much. 'Quant'e?'

He seems very happy that I've caught on. 'Cinque Euro,' comes the reply, along with a small bar receipt.

I pull out the cash from my wallet after yet more fidgeting and hand it to him, along with a Euro extra, just to be sporting. He nods contentedly and walks back into the gloomy, internal bar. In Italy if you don't leave a tip, it's just not cricket. Or *that pointless English teadrinking sport,* as my friends refer to it.

Once again I relax in the creaky seat - to a noise which sounds like a mix between a fart and a toad croaking - and set about savouring my breakfast. It's the most important meal of the day. I'm using the milk in the latte to line my poor, battered stomach and replace some of the protein I cold-heartedly executed last night. My organs must be thinking I've declared war on them - one day I'll be up on charges at the Hague. The wine, sitting as yet untouched on the table, is phase four of the hangover process and will help 'counteract' the effects of last nights alcohol by essentially keeping me pissed. Rustic remedies aside, I actually enjoy the tepid coffee and in three large gulps it's gone, working its way into my desperate body.

As I set the cup down a pair of attractive

women in their early twenties walk past the terrace. Both of them have dark hair, dark eyes, bronzed skin and I smile as they pass me. One of them smiles back and even goes a step further, taking a good look back over her shoulder before turning to her friend and whispering into a cupped hand. I watch with interest as they pass the three men on the table in front. All of them, without exception, stop talking and almost offensively look the women up and down as they pass. As the women go round a corner and out of sight, the men nudge each other, make some sotto-voce comments and burst out laughing again.

Revelling in the little ego boost, a sip of wine goes down very nicely and I suddenly realise just how well this year is shaping up. Don't get me wrong it started badly, really badly. Back on that piss wet, Winter's day when Claire left me I couldn't see how all the coin tossing in the world would make things better. I could just see myself in a right mess because of her. In the end though, I'm not even bitter about it - in fairness she did me a huge favour. She spurred me into action and I began the process of taking my life to pieces and rebuilding it, with all the bad stuff removed.

I was overcome by the urge to edit everything around me and started by burning the bed we'd slept in together. Call it symbolic if you will but I've always been a bit of pyromaniac, so I love an excuse for a fire. I can attribute this to my grandfather, nicknamed Spludger - he once brought tractor tyres with him to help my then teenage brothers build what he called a 'proper bonfire'. Unbelievably, the same man was a fireman during the war, which may explain why so much of Southampton was destroyed. With the bed burning being the start of it all, the next thing I did was revisit my coin tossing. I phoned some people - lots of them - and a couple of months later my house was on the market.

When I bought that house, my first home, six years ago it was a bit dilapidated and cost me thirty-nine thousand pounds. I tinkered with it, changed things, re-jigged the kitchen and loved living there. Claire spent a lot of her time there too but it was always my place and she never moved in fully. Even then, I now see, it was like she was holding back, just in case. I guess she was just securing her escape route in case she had to cut and run one day. After we split, the house felt a bit tarnished and, even though it was mine, there was something about us in every room. Something we'd chosen, or chipped or scuffed. Something we'd done together. In the end I just couldn't stand it.

I never imagined all my tinkering would mean the house went up in value at anything beyond inflation. When the agents first came round I thought they were way off the mark but it sold. This was two months ago and it went, in the end, for one hundred and thirty-nine thousand pounds after being on the market at three thousand pounds more. I spent the week after completion fixated with checking my bank balance. Just shy of one-hundred thousand pounds sounds fantastic when read out by a recorded voice on the end of a phone.

With the house gone it was out with the old and in with the new and that is how I've eventually ended up here. Sardegna. Or Sardinia to the Brits. I've never understood, why we change the name of a place to our own language. Surely the place name should remain exactly the same? It's like saying my name can't be Jack in France, it must be Jacques; or here in Italy, Giacomo.

Sardegna, Sardinia - I think we'll go native and stick with Sardegna - is a large island to the west of mainland Italy, way above Sicily and just barely detached from Corsica. I'm not big on Geography, so I'm not going to explain the physical structure of the place or population densities. Let's just say it's beautiful. The beaches blow me away and there's always something new to find. A mountain, a village, a cove you can only get to by boat. Christ the place is awesome. It has problems, though, employment being one, but tell me a place that doesn't? I feel just as safe walking around the southern city of Cagliari at four in the morning as I do at four in the afternoon, it's a million miles away from the life I've just ditched. The dangers of drunken idiots on Friday and Saturday nights don't exist here. The streets are not a war zone.

It's not the first time I've been here. I didn't just pluck it out of thin air as a destination. Before Claire, my first proper girlfriend was Italian and she brought me here two years on the bounce. I even picked up the lingo and made some friends on the way. As for that particular ex, the last I heard she was living in America and married to a banker.

By this point, though, I was so much in love with the place that, even afterwards, I used to bring Claire with me every year. I maintained the friendships I had made. They've even been over to England to visit - two of them were at my place within a week of Claire leaving as they knew I needed it. They're experts in cheering me up, like they've been specifically trained for it. They are the green beret wearing, commandos of mirth and frivolity. All in all I've been coming here for about nine years but this time is totally different. No going back.

I've told my boss to stick his job where the sun don't shine - I think it's called England - and packed up everything I own. I've come to start over. I really am a brave little soldier. From house move to hangover, I'm fearless. Or mental. Or both. The day I sat on the cold tiles in my old kitchen, that's what the coin toss was for. Should I stay or should I go. Chase the dream for once, or wait around for it to chase me.

Two last, relaxing gulps finish off the Vermentino and already I'm feeling much more like last-night's self. I suppose, at some point, somebody will make me eat but for the moment I'm happy to let the light-headed feeling creep over me. The three Italian lads are finishing off their drinks and standing up.

'Andamus?' says the ringleader. This is followed by thoughtful looks by the others before they reply. He stares at both of them almost impatiently. I get the impression he wasn't so much asking a question, as giving an order.

I've noticed it's quite common to find hierarchy features like this, particularly in groups of Italian men.

'Aio,' comes the first, thoughtful reply.

'Eja,' follows and all three appear to be in agreement.

With that, bank notes are thrown on the table and they walk away, into the bright glare of the sun. I suddenly realise from this last snippet why I couldn't follow their conversation. They were speaking in Nuorese. It's a language all on its own, from the centre of the island. I'd love to learn it properly, rather than just swear words and general make-you-laugh stuff I know now. That will be a task for the future, as my Italian is far from perfect. While my accent is fine and I can babble away for hours, grammar and tenses are a problem. I guess learning most of it while drunk or laughing hasn't helped. However, I can get by and I'm getting better every day. Total immersion therapy is what I call it and it's working a treat.

I put two and two together and work out that 'andamus' must be the same as 'andiamo' - let's go - in Italian. The other two words are just little affirmative responses. These can be filed - complete with pronunciation 'aye-oh' and 'ey-ah' - for future reference. In fact, I'll use them to mix things up a little and, as an added bonus it'll make my friends chuckle.

With that I my phone vibrates. It's a text message from Lella. 'Dove' cazzo sei?' *Where the dick are you?* Italians use the word dick rather than fuck in conversation - just a useful tid-bit of information I've picked up. I love the little differences.

**

Admittedly, even by my standards, arriving at the beach at this time is not only poor form but might well inhibit my ability to acquire a tan - which, for me, means more of a bright red glow. Walking along the scrub land with the incredibly bumpy, dirt track running alongside - where Italian drivers carelessly smash their cars along at the start and end of the beach day - I look out at the pristine water. Turquoise on the shore line where it gently caresses the bright red and dark blue pebbles, becoming a deeper blue green. The two colours swirl simultaneously rather than mixing, as the sea moves out into the flat cove. It's a mill pond and I love it. Am in awe of it. Even if I am late.

I can see my friends, just ahead and growing larger as I slowly cover the distance to our usual spot. Our claimed land. The sound of their voices carries easily, effortlessly, in the still heat. Daniele I can clearly make out - bald head the give away - lying on his stomach asleep, as he normally is at the beach. Occasionally he gets flipped by one of us, to even out his colour. Enrico is at Daniele's side, resting his head on the crossed legs of Roberta. Both of them are stacking stones in the centre of Daniele's back, creating a circular tower of pebbles. Clearly recognisable to all Sardinians, it is a Nuraghe - or at least a model of one of the Bronze Age buildings which stand proud across the island. Some, such as those at

Barumini, grew into large, complex citadels, where water was worshipped.

Lella, is kneeling by Daniele's feet, fumbling in her handbag. I smile as their laughter carries, washes over me as the sun warms my face and the lapping water pleases my eyes. The dull fuzz of the second Vermentino sits pleasantly in control of all of this.

'Aió Lella, che se si sveglia, lo rovina!' Roberta almost shouts. *Come on, if he wakes up he'll ruin it.* Still fumbling through her bag, a common sight due to the sheer size of it and the amount of crap she carries around with her, Lella finally pulls the digital camera out.

'Se si sveglia dagli un colpo!' Laughing and turning the camera on, she tells Roberta to knock him out if he wakes up.

Enrico calmly and gently places a final stone on top of the Nuraghe and poses. 'Questa foto verrá prodotta in molteplice copia ed incorniciata.' I'm copying and framing this, he says proudly.

'Pronti?' *Ready?* says Lella, pointing the Camera. I see Daniele absently swat a fly away from his face and hear a loud, nasal, half snore escape. He sounds like a bear and the current adornment to his spine suits his Neanderthal appearance and mannerisms. I've often thought we could make a fortune, selling him as a live exhibit to one of the Natural History Museums.

'Veloci!' Roberta squeals. *Quick!*

With the photo taken my three friends collapse about laughing. I am about to quicken my pace, to cover the last metres, when I stop in my tracks and gawk - yes, a proper, slack jawed gawk. Monia walks out of the water, glistening with beads of it as she crosses the short slice of beach to join the others. She is beaming, perfect.

'State di nuovo rompendo le scatole all'uomo delle caverne?' *Are you breaking the caveman's balls again?* She walks around Daniele, standing over him at the head end of the towel. As this is happening, I notice a curious thing, rather than translate what's being said into an English thought, I am just understanding it as it is.

'Well, we couldn't make a sand castle, so we went with Nuraghe...creative aren't we?' Enrico cranes his head up from Roberta's leg, talking to Monia.

'I'll show you the picture when you're dry, definitely one for the fridge!' laughs Lella, again fumbling around in her bag for something.

'I'll never hear the end of it,' mutters Roberta, in the knowledge Daniele is prone to lasting grumps.

As if to confirm this, Daniele grunt-snores and swats at his nose again. Bizarrely it reminds me of a hippo. With that, Monia, still standing over Daniele, leans forward, and rings her long hair out, water splashing down onto his head and shoulders. In the constant heat, even at this hour, his baked skin must have received quite a surprise.

'Che cazzo!?' Daniele roars. Lumbering into a kneeling position, the stone building collapsing on his back and thudding onto his legs and towel, he shakes his head and repeats the expletive.

'Caveman by name...' Enrico roars with friendly laughter and Roberta reaches across and touches Daniele's forearm, even from this distance you can see a soft caress.

'What's the matter honey? Did you hear a mammouth coming?' He glowers at her and Lella captures the moment perfectly with another click of the camera.

'Perfect, that's two to send, as proof of life, to the Discovery Channel,' she chips in, then resumes fumbling, much as I imagine Mary Poppins would when looking for a pack of mints amongst floor lamps.

Daniele looks up at Monia, an almost pleading look, the request for assistance clear upon his face. 'Isn't my little sister going to defend me from these cretins?'

She giggles and points at Roberta. 'If your fiancée isn't going to, don't look at me for help!' With a further twist of her hair, she flicks more water at him.

'Basta!' he bellows - *Stop!* - with that launching himself at his sister and chasing her to the water's edge, where he picks her up and jumps in, drenching both of them. Monia is screaming happily all the way and the others laugh along.

My phone rings in my pocket and I fish it out. It's Lella, having finally found her mobile. She starts to ask where the dick I am, then sees me standing a short distance away and hangs up, shaking her head. I'd forgotten I was standing still, watching the scene rather than joining in, so cover the ground sharpish and find myself subject to an immediate, Italian barrage.

'Christ, did you want to leave it any later?' Enrico.

'The mess you were in last night, I'm surprised you aren't still in bed!' Lella.

'If you had come any earlier, you'd have been burned bright red by now!' Roberta.

'He'll be bright red when he sees Monia, do you remember last time?' Enrico.

'We had to pull them apart last time!' Roberta.

'I can't blame her, he is kind of attractive' Lella.

'I'll sell you to him if you like?' Enrico.

'You're jealous really, when I have babies I want them to have his eyes!' Roberta.

Working together in quick fire rounds like this, I find them hard to follow but I am no shrinking violet, no wall flower. I am just as fearless piping up, as I am when it comes to going to the toilet. 'Vuoi I miei occhi? Credo d'avere un cucchiaio qua dentro la borsa,' I tug my battered rucksack from my shoulders and sling it down by my feet, then unzip it, imitating Lella and searching. *You want my eyes? I'm sure I have a spoon here somewhere.*

Roberta reaches across and slaps my leg gently. 'Ciao bello!' She says, as I lean down and kiss her on each cheek.

'Ciao Sbobby!' I say which, roughly translated, means hello you disgusting mess. The word for mess is sbobba and at some point, invariably while completely leathered, I combined this with Bobby. A true, master wordsmith aren't I? Roberta is, in reality, far from a disgusting mess.

Enrico stands up, shakes my hand and kisses me on the cheek. 'Hello little drain, how are you?' *Pozzetto* has been my name, one of them, for a while. A testament to my ability, to make drink and food disappear at will and without apparent limit. The next name up the scale in Italian is suitcase, *valigia*. An item of some capacity, designed to be filled.

'I got promoted from pozzetto to valigia, didn't I tell you?' I ask my friend.

'Never mind suitcase, you my friend are so much more!' his reply is immediate and as he says this Lella pounces on me, kissing my cheeks and lips, arms wrapped around my neck and dragging me to my knees.

'So much more! Never mind valigia, you are a valiJack!'

'Perfect!' Enrico claps his hands, laughing, 'valiJack!'

I am a little miffed by this, making up nicknames, sopranomi, is pretty much my job. I say this sulkily and Lella immediately picks up on this faux hurt.

'Now that you've been promoted, you can delegate!' I laugh and turn my attentions to Enrico.

'Did I hear you say you would sell her to me?' I whisper, in the best conspirational tone I can muster. It isn't very good if I am brutally honest.

'Yeah, I guess so...fifty euros?'

'You pair of utter bastards, I am worth at least one hundred!' Lella half growls, slapping the pair of us hard enough to generate swears.

As I was saying, I've known these reprobates, except Roberta, since the first year I came here. They were my ex's school friends and now they are my grownup friends. It's Funny how life does this sometimes and, despite the obvious violence, they are a good bunch. Lella and Enrico have been together since those school days and, I suppose, one day they'll get married. In the meantime, Enrico's always trying to sell her to his friends. Or anyone it seems. Roberta is engaged to Daniele, they met two years ago and fell in love. Well, he fell in love, I'm not quite sure what her defect is.

After a brief, Lellaesque fumble in my bag, I unwrap my towel and spread it out, getting comfy just as Daniele resurfaces from the sea, greeting me with a wet handshake even as I take off my t-shirt. With drips of cold, salt water splattering against my skin, which is embarrassingly pale by comparison to his, he leans down and kisses me on the cheek. 'Ciao Roast Beef, novita?' *What's new?*

'Mild hangover, no sex.'

'Same as me then,' he replies. This is swiftly followed by a yelp, as Roberta punches him, hard, on the leg. 'Merda!' he exclaims, rubbing the side of his thigh. 'Chiama la pula!' *Call the rozzers!*

'I'll give you some domestic violence...' Smiling sweetly up at Daniele, Roberta flutters her eyes and sucks a fingertip.

'Right, we're going,' Daniele replies, without hesitation. A clear look of immediate lust upon his face.

'Puzzo?' I say, raising my arm and sniffing my armpit.

'No,' he says, dragging Roberta to her feet and quickly gathering up their beach towels, 'but when sex is offered...carpe momentum.'

I laugh at this. 'I'll see you later then!'

'We'll call you in a couple of hours,' Enrico adds, curiously watching the Neanderthal as he aggressively jams items into Roberta's beach bag, all speed and no panache.

'Let's not exaggerate, call us in fifteen minutes,' Roberta replies, slapping Daniele on the buttocks.

'And that includes the ten it takes you to get home,' Lella giggles.

'É una malattia!' Daniele scowls - *it's a medical condition* - then turns to Enrico. 'Can you give Monia a lift for me?'

I cough, loudly, attracting his attention

while looking about as angelic as Lucifer.

Glowering at me, brow furrowed, he says 'Do you know Steven Seagal?' then raises his hands, snapping imaginary limbs in two and generating a rather realistic crack noise from his closed mouth. 'Togli le zampe da mia sorella!' He finishes. *Keep your paws off my sister.*

'Come on Neanderthal, stop picking on foreigners and take me back to our cave,' Roberta says, idly twisting a lock of hair.

Without further speech, Daniele grunts, picks her up, slings her over his shoulder, and sets off up the beach. Roberta waves, laughing hysterically.

'The man is an animal!' Enrico says, shaking his head and smiling.

'Told you, he's a caveman. We have more than enough evidence,' Lella says, taking a photo of the departing pair, Daniele covering the sand at quite some pace.

I silently empathise with his needs as Monia is stepping out of the water, body glistening again in the now lower sun. She pads softly towards us and stands over me, water splashing my legs and torso. I smile up at her. God she looks good.

'What, no kiss?' I say.

'Oh you want a kiss do you?' She pouts and places her hands on her hips.

Enrico leans toward Lella, placing his hand in front of her face. 'Lella, shield your delicate eyes!'

She bats him away, stands up and drags him to his feet. 'Time for us to go too,' she says, smirking. 'Can you give Monia a lift home?' She winks as she says it, scoops up the two beach towels and ridiculous bag, grabs Enrico by the hand and leads him off without opportunity to do anything but wave.

'Grazie! Not embarrassing at all!' I call after them, the last in English - a language I now use once a week, when calling my parents. I look back to Monia, still standing, still glistening, still pouting down at me.

She speaks softly but with a direct tone I find utterly irrestible. 'Ma allora il bacio lo vuoi?' *So do you want this kiss then?*

'Beh...' I say, shrugging my shoulders. *Well...*

Without further warning she dives on me,

giggling and showering my face with elaborately noisy, smacking kisses. I am powerless to resist and collapse back on the towel, her astride me and still kissing away. I resort to tickling, she shrieks and rolls off.

As the laughter naturally and comfortably subsides, we find ourselves lying on my towel, facing each other on propped elbows. She looks truly stunning, stroking the hair away from her face. My heart is racing, my breath quick. There has always been something there, ever since we first met. The feeling of attraction seemed to be mutual and was practically rabid when I was with Claire, driven by want being multiplied when you can't. Or shouldn't.

'Carpe momentum,' I whisper.

BUGABOO

"Ye have heard of the patience of Job":

Nestled among the crisp and often black framed frontages of the Savile Row tailors, stood a set of the most apparently uninteresting railings. A small gap in this bland ironwork would lead any curious person down a set of plain, grey, stone steps to a crisply lacquered door of oak, with a spectacular ivory knocker. This otherwise unpretentious looking basement with the extraordinary door furniture hides behind it one of Savile Row's best tailors.

Hides may not be the just word however, it doesn't quite convey the exclusivity of the client list. Men with real power tap the ivory against the pristine, English wood; men with unimaginable wealth tread those plain, grey, stone steps. Despite all of this the master tailor, Emery Porter-Gladstone, is never phased, never loses composure and is, at all times, utterly dignified and unflappable. That is to say, Emery Porter-Gladstone is all of those things, to all men, at all times, with the exception of today. He was feeling the heat, quite literally, thanks to some kind of unfathomable hiccup with his central heating system and it simply wouldn't do.

His client stood patiently, smiling good humouredly into his own image, reflected in the full length mirror proudly placed next to the huge, white fireplace with ebony detailing running across the mantle. A tall, slim man wearing a superbly cut suit – to Emery's horror it had a Boston tailor's name stitched into the inside of the watch pocket – he smiled placidly at the tailor too and that same, good humour practically sparkled in his eyes. The heat didn't seem to be affecting him yet, which was good as Emery was bothered enough for both of them, feeling increasingly mortified - his very Britishness amplifying the sentiment tenfold. It seemed to him things had gone wrong from the minute this client had walked in.

"I am so terribly sorry about this heating fiasco, it simply won't do." Flustered and sweating, Emery set about his measurements, finding his unusual feelings of anxiousness, of being flapped, increased to a point of being almost unbearable every time he got close enough to touch his client.

The client smiled and looked at Emery in a most curious fashion, his dark eyes seemed to swim with all the glee of a pool of hungry sharks. "It's really no problem." The client spoke with a broad, Texan accent which grated in the otherwise quiet suite of Porter-Gladstone, "And for Christ's sakes, call me Nick would you?."

The dilaect was one which Emery particularly disliked in any case but, at the mention of the word Christ, it had the exact effect of nails being drawn on a blackboard, causing a physical shudder beyond his control. "I must be coming down with a touch of the influenza."

Emery only realised he had said this aloud when the Texan replied, watching him curiously, with a disturbing amount of apparent mirth stemming from his obvious discomfort. "You look Devilish ill, I must say. You should lie down." The blackness of his eyes swam and Emery found himself stuck to the spot, with the heat in the room growing more fierce. The Texan reached out towards him, his slender hand moving in the direction the tailor's shoulder then, suddenly, dropped it back by his side and sighed, heavily. "I think my old friend has arrived."

Emery shook his head, as a man waking from a trance, and could not remember exactly what had happened, the question mark he wore on his otherwise distinguished face a testament to this. Looking at his client, he found the broad smile the Texan sported was, apparently, cringe-inducing and flinched away from it, eyes darting around the room in obvious confusion. No shadow had passed the window facing the steps, Emery's time served mechanism for identifying the arrival of custom. Yet, with that, the door knocked and Emery jumped.

"Right on time," the client said, his smile now so broad it looked as though his head might split in two, become a giant mouth, and devour everything nearby, Emery included. Emery, with great relish.

The door knocked a second time, another of Emery's golden rules, his proudly held traditions, broken in the space of one morning. He broke away from Nick - having a pallid look of Feta cheese about him - and found he actually scurried to the door, like a field-mouse under the eyes of a hawk.

The door opened on a young man, half the age of the Texan, slim, blonde-haired with piercing blue eyes and a solemn, pained look on his face. He was wearing incredibly ripped jeans and a t-shirt - a most distasteful print of the Turin Shroud which looked as if it could stand up on it's own. In a final horror, at least to the experienced eyes of Savile Row, he cast his eyes down and saw bare, filthy feet. A tramp! In all his years no tramps had ventured down these steps, Emery Porter-Gladstone began to shut the door, then stopped.

"Am I welcome?" said a soft, boy's voice. Emery came over hot and cold at once, his face towards the unpleasantly grimy newcomer becoming almost ice cold, while his back felt as if it were on fire. "Am I welcome?" The young man repeated.

"For God's sake Em," the Texan boomed, causing Emery to lurch on his feet. "Don't keep my oldest friend out there all day."

Emery slumped forwards and the world wobbled, but he held the solid oak, took strength from it and, somehow, managed to regain some semblance of proper composure. "Ah...of course...come in, come in, please take a seat." He swept his hand in the direction of a comfortable couch, facing the fitting area, the mirror, and the mantle. A place where he positioned his clients, kings among men, so the anticipation of their own fitting could build as they watched this tailor of renown do his work.

The young man sat down, stretching his arms over the seat back and opened his legs in a most ungentlemanly pose. Emery immediately began to mentally seek the name of an upholsterer, to replace the tarnished fabric and, as he did, the room started to cool down. "I think your heating is on the blink," he said. "It's a bit chilly in here." His boy's voice a curious, pure British accent of no place in particular. He turned from Emery to focus on the Texan. "Are you up to mischief? Old tricks?." The Texan didn't turn to face the young man himself, but watched him in the mirror, some of the previous glee seeming to dribble away. Oh my Lord, a drugs deal, that's what this is, Emery thought to himself being only too aware that many of his clients had a penchant for recreational cocaine.

"Don't worry Em, this isn't a drug deal," the Texan said, still not turning to face the arrival he had apparently invited.

"Stop playing with the man."

The voice from the sofa caused Emery to pause with his tape, just when he had been about to resume measurements. He glanced up at the Texan, who touched him on the shoulder, the same shoulder he had reached for only minutes ago. Emery Porter-Gladstone, with that, dropped dead and lay on the floor in a disappointingly untidy heap. Neither of the other men so much as moved.

"So," Nick said, still talking to the reflection of the ruffian on the sofa, "has it been that long already?"

The younger man rose, crossed the room to stand behind the Texan, and placed both hands on his shoulders, staring keenly into the eyes of the reflection. This caused a scream, a guttural roar of pleasure and pain, before the younger man let go. "The number of souls tells me too long, old Nick." He began to pad slowly around the tailor's suite, careful to step over the body of Emery, where it lay.

"The number of souls is because they just don't listen to your word any more. Or is it just that your word doesn't have the power it once did. How is your soul count recently?" Nick spoke boldly but stuttered at the last, almost a sharp intake of breath, as if he had said too much. Gone too far.

"The problem with my word has always been the way it's been interpreted by man. Subsequently, although they frequently question my word, they should take a little look beyond their own ego's and see they've not paid enough attention. Take Moses, did I say go and get lost for a long time? No, he just didn't listen to my directions well enough. It's when I have to use a prophet and he doesn't quite get it right the problems begin. It's the grandest scale of Chinese whispers." The younger man spoke absently, as if this was an often repeated conversation. "I've even given them a huge sign post by making 'the Devil is in the detail' a famous saying. It's true, that is where the Devil lives and when one of the details I give is missed, ignored, or misinterpreted, no matter how small that detail is, the Devil will seize on it and exaggerate its impact. He waits to pounce on misinterpretation and uses man's corruption of my word to his own ends." He jumped on the sofa, then jumped down again, leaving black footprints.

"After all this time, you still call me *He*? You know I get the point, but have you considered appearing in a more awe inspiring form and doing the job yourself?" the Texan replied, glaring into the mirror at first then sighing, softening and shrugging his shoulders before moving on to a marginally different topic. He had been down this road several times and knew the answer by the heart he didn't have. "Somewhere on the internet the Lutherans have tried to give you a nickname...they've gone for Trinity as it's easier than The Father, Son and Holy Spirit."

The young man shook his head, still padding barefoot, stepping over the corpse again as he circuited the room. "Well that's like saying the word pâté and missing the accent on the *e*. Technically it's the same thing but it misses the very vital little element which makes it what it is. Pah-tay is pâté. You might as well call it peight. Still tastes okay but you've just alienated half the market who love the French heritage and linked imagery. It would be a PR disaster. Pâté's easier to sell and if the Lutherans knew how competitive the marketplace has become they wouldn't try and peddle the other!"

Nick watched the pacing via the mirror, trying to judge the mood before replying.

This was the first face-to-face conversation they had had in a very long time. "Your problem is scruples. I, on the other hand, am quite happy to sell cod roe as caviar and still sleep easy. You created a race that is easily confused and misled."

The pacing stopped and those eyes were on his reflection. Had it been a direct stare a whole universe of righteous fury would have withered him to dust. In that he drew a little satisfaction. "If you'd like to see confused just take a look at omnipotence on Wikipedia. Round and round, none of them knowing the answer or even interested in giving it. The main aim seems to be to 'out-clever' each other. Again it's a case of man being too smart for his own good, on a website that your lot have made Nick! I mean, seriously, I searched the problem of evil...", a sigh followed. "It was a good suggestion by you all those years ago to throw in the concept that evil doesn't actually exist. How many party invites have you managed off the back of that?"

"We'll, I am now welcome in many circles of power and wealth, more so than ever before. I'm here visiting a few at parliament as it happens."

"You know what the problem is, when you directly compare the faith of a poor person and a rich person?" Nick knew this rhetoric perfectly. "Well, if a poor man has nothing and expects nothing and God gives him a twig, he goes from having nothing to something and is grateful, just because he has gone from a poor man with nothing to a poor man with something – in this case a twig." The pacing resumed. "If a rich person who has lots gets something else, they come to expect and accept that is the way it is and are not grateful. If anything they become ungrateful. When a rich person has lots and does not get anything else, in their eyes they become a rich person without something. You may think the door may be opened wider to the Devil by the poor man with nothing but the lack of expectation acts like a chain and keeps him - or *you*, seeing as he causes such offence - out."

Nick was delighted and this time could simply not contain it, letting out a deep, rumbling laugh. "So, there we are. All this time to repeat the same old bet. How is Job these days?" The young man ignored this and stared, now standing still once more, at the reflection which had started to bend and warp into true form. Nick hung his head, quieted once more.

"My thoughts are these: I will test someone again and this time, depressed as I am with the state of things, if you win, if they falter in their love and faith, then the world is yours to deal with as we long discussed. I did, after all, create you for that very purpose and have held you off only through constant changes of heart and hope about humanity."

Nick snapped his head upright and peered into the reflected, pale blue eyes. The same truth was there as always had been. What a curious being – one who could make worlds but not lie. For one designed to tell untruths it was an impossible to decipher enigma. "And if you win?"

"If I win..." The young man paused once more. "Then, Lucifer, you may come home." The last was met with silence, utter silence of the kind in which pins can heard dropping on carpeted floors. The Devil stood stock-still, dumbfounded by his creator. To coin a phrase, struck dumb by the voice of God. "I'll be in touch, I have someone and something in mind, but first, please leave."

Old Nick, as he was today - a dapper, show

boating Texan - nodded then, with that, disappeared completely, suit and all. The young man knelt, touching Emery lightly on the forearm and wandered slowly out. The door closed softly behind him, ivory tapping gently on the oak as it shut.

Emery Porter-Gladstone telephoned his clients, those booked for the rest of the day, and, making profuse apologies about his serious and unexpected bout of the flu, did something for the first time in years. He closed early. He was miserable that his morning client hadn't turned up - a typical show-boating Texan: all volume and no substance - and, troubled by his passing out, went home to sleep.

His nightmares lasted until his scheduled death not so long afterwards.

"God is love":

"Yeah....well why don't you fuck off and die slowly, you gilt-edged, double-barreled fuckstick." The phone slammed down and all was silent once more, aside from Frank's agitated, furious panting.

Jack quietly set his coffee down on the kitchen worktop in the house he had grown up in. Once bursting with chatter and the smells of cakes and cheese straws, it was now silent and washed out. Heartless, since the death of his mother.

He walked into the hall and looked at his Dad, his once immortal father who now just looked like an old man. "Pops, I can find the money. They can't just throw you out." The conversation with the mortgage company had not gone so well, they had lost patience.

It wasn't Frank's fault. He had to give up work, after a life with the rarest of days off, to care for his dying wife. They received no housing benefit, no council tax relief and, after the savings were gone, that was that. After Georgie died he had tried to find work but was too old, his experience counting for nothing in the current climate because it came with a certain expectation of pay. "Son," Frank said, then fell to the floor as the blood filled balloon, nestled in his Circle of Willis, burst.

"Yes, an aneurysm...straight after your phone call...I don't want your sympathy...can't you just delay another week...please? PLEASE?...rot in hell!" Jack, mirroring his father's last moments, slammed down the telephone, this time in his own, modest studio. In the land of mortgage collections death is meaningless. He had no choice but to empty his parents house by the weekend.

Shaking he picked the phone up again and dialled the number for his manager. "Pete, I have to take the rest of the week off...no...I have to empty the house by the weekend...there is no other way. Are you taking the fucking piss?Sorry? SORRY? FUCK YOU!" He slammed the phone down again, this time jobless.

"I've paid tax and National Insurance since I was sixteen. I've worked - a concept which most of the clientele in here don't seem to get - full time since I was seventeen and, thirteen years down the road, you sit there and tell me I don't qualify for benefits?"

Behind the counter the civil servant, a lifetime of listening to excuses, lies, and sad stories, did not flinch. Simply blowing her nose and nodding. "We can't keep going through this, you don't meet the new criteria."

"Well, in that case," Jack said as he stood up,

trembling with rage and tearing his paperwork into pieces, "I'd best fuck off before I do something I'll regret." The woman sat placidly as the torn papers showered around her like snowflakes.

"Mrs Sampson, Eileen...please, two more days, I have nowhere to go." Pleading with his landlady was now futile. Her son loomed in the doorway of the furnished flat they were evicting him from, just a kit bag full of clothes to his name having pawned his belongings (and those of his parents) to pay the last three months rent and food. Eileen shook her head, confirming his opinion that she was a hard faced bitch. Her son reached towards Jack. "I really fucking wouldn't." Unsure, uncertain, the man withdrew his hand.

Jack pushed past him, down the stairs and out into the street. The chill of November bit straight away but he walked quickly, angry tears stinging his cheeks as night began to fall. He paused at the cashpoint, next to the pub with heaters out the front. The two men were watching him closely.

"Gabe, I think the old man has finally lost it. That boy is no more than one step from a trip downstairs," said the imp, who was as old as time.

Gabriel looked at him with eyes of such pale blue they appeared almost white. Loki was, irritatingly right and for an archangel to even acknowledge this thought was dangerous. "God is cruel, it's a rule that's even older than you." he said, swirling the ice cubes in his mojito. "Not, of course, that you are so bothered about upstairs or downstairs. You were a cast off. An accident left in limbo."

"An accident?" Loki roared with laughter, as only the Norse 'God' of mischief can. "You make me sound like the kind of accident a child has after Lucifer takes his weekly tour of the dreams of man."

Gabriel sighed, the imp was hitting all the right notes. "Accident isn't the right word, you're right." Loki was a *biproduct* of creation.

When God created the world, like any potter at the wheel, there was some degree of mess. The problem arose because God loves all his creations, even those he didn't intend. The California Sheephead being a prime example. Essentially, when he was seeding Eden, some of the mess landed on an empty piece of land where God, out of curiosity, watched to see what it grew into. The end result was Loki. Of course, the good Lord couldn't admit to having done it in error, because that would make him fallible, so he accepted the existence and blessed him with eternal life. However, the caveat was Loki could not be part of the Eden Project, as it is now called in the quieter circles of Heaven.

At first this wasn't such a problem but Loki got lonely and began to cause a nuisance. This distracted God and that's how the apple tree incident happened. Eve did exactly what humans do when they think no one is watching them. Following this, the continents got moved and Loki was given some very specific boundaries about where he could appear. He had to wait, alone and effectively on God's version of the naughty step, for thousands of years while humanity repeated the original sin and spread across the Earth.

In the meantime, the war in Heaven had taken it's toll and Lucifer was cast down into the bowels of the earth. The conflict hadn't been strictly necessary, as Lucifer had been created to fulfil this role, but God felt it was needed in order to underline the concept evil was bad. After all, he couldn't lie. So there had to be truth in the story of Heaven and Hell. With all this going on, Loki was momentarily forgotten - with moments lasting for millennia - and, where the intention had been to pop him into the first circle of Hell (that later shown to Dante as Limbo) the door was shut before it could be done. This lead to an issue, because only the souls of the dead could enter Hell and Loki had been blessed with eternal life. God, of course, never goes back on his word.

Gabriel sighed again.

"I do prefer the Dogma story of my creation." Loki liked to peddle that he was a fallen angel and he, with his friend Bartleby, were seeking a route back to heaven.

"How many people have you taken in with that now?"

"You'd be surprised at how few know Bartelby was a scrivener, invented by Dickens."

"Don't you ever get bored of it?"

"Never, not a once. Man is the child from the other side of the fence, the one I can only play with when no one is watching because my dad will go crazy." Loki knew full well God would not do anything of the sort. After naughty-stepping him that once, he had let Loki be. He could steal no souls and not influence any actions of evil, only make man feel stupid through mischief and trickery which, being a fallacy from the outset, held no weight in Peter's decisions at the gate. Loki knew that Gabe knew this, thus proving the point.

"I doesn't feel right, doing this next bit."

"So don't do it!"

"You know I can't disobey his word" replied Gabriel. Quite rightly too. Aside from the angels God had made specifically to be rebellious in order that Hell could be created, all other angels were created to carry out the word of God implicitly. Question the word, yes, providing they were archangels, disobey the word? Absolutely impossible.

"And what exactly is the word of God, in this case?." Loki raised his eyebrow and smirked.

"On this occasion it is to let him get to the end of the street, then have three young men rob him at knife point."

"I thought Daddy was all about love?"

"God is love."

"But God is cruel, you said only moments ago!" Looking increasingly amused by Gabe's obvious discomfort, Loki continued. "So is he cruel or is he love?"

Gabriel swirled his ice cubes. "Love is cruel. You have to be cruel to be kind. Love hurts. Why do these expressions exist? It's because they are true, the word of God in general use. In order to feel love you must feel pain because, without pain, you will not appreciate love and not ask for it. Not believe that you will one day feel it. That's the fundamental basis of faith. The craving, the desire to feel that love, normally manifested or found once again during times of extreme cruelty or pain."

"Faith is the hope of love," Loki sighed, understanding it from a personal perspective.

Gabriel eyed him and would have smiled if he could. Instead he placed his glass down on the table and stood up, without a further word. It was time.

"I have to go too," said Loki glancing at the young man walking up the street, shoulders slumped. He saw his own, eternal years reflected. "I have to set up some troll accounts on Twitter."

"Mischief of the new world," Gabriel muttered, then stepped onto the pavement and paced slowly up the street without looking back.

Loki watched him briefly then walked in the opposite direction.

DANGEROUS IDEAS

1st of May 2034

The screams rose into a guttural, animal like shriek, then were replaced by a more palatable, gargling rasp as the vocal chords burned away and the man's head caught fire. The flaming body underneath it stopped making forward steps, knelt, and fell forwards with a dull thud.

"Shit!" shouted Tom in the quiet street, the only real noise the sound of human fat softly spitting as it cooked.

He had a nice smile, Tom. Subject to many a compliment, by many a woman, and he wore it broadly as he stepped toward the charring lump. The straps of his flame thrower tanks creaked as he leaned slightly forwards, lifting the visor of his police helmet. He spat on the body and it sizzled. He laughed to himself, spat once more and turned around. The bullet struck him clean on the bridge of the nose, driving through his face, splintering bones as it battered into his skull, mushrooming and changing direction before tearing out of the back of his head. Eventually it came to a dead stop against the impact attenuating Kevlar of the inside of the helmet.

He made no sound, no shrieks. He just fell backwards, as if in a faint, his pack hitting the floor with a clang, the hose rupturing at the joint, fuel spilling and running on the camber of the road. It crossed the few feet to the burning corpse in seconds. Tom exploded seconds after that, a much bigger fireball lighting up the street. Pieces of him clattered and splattered across every nearby surface, some alight, some smoking. Some raw.

In that flash I could see my reflection in the remaining half of a shop window. The black clothing, black armour, black helmet, black boots. The gun in my hand, dropped by my side. The pale, almost bright white face behind the perspex visor. I could see a ghost.

I'm glad I shot him. Tom. He'd been enjoying this too much lately. With each new generation it seems that they have become more equipped to deal with it. I will never be able to do so, because I remember how things were. How they should be still. I'm getting too old for this and Tom, a probationer in old-speak, was just at the beginning. By the time he reached my level of service what on earth would he be prepared to do?

As I did on many a turbulent night since it all changed, I found myself wishing more than ever I'd had the balls to do something about it, in the there and then. I stepped closer to the window, in the grim here and now, my choice hovering over my soul like a vulture and, as the fire died back down, I saw it had been a book shop. Nothing much was there now, most of it taken for winter fuel. Nothing but a carelessly torn section of a book, wedged under a breeze block. Presumably the one which had broken the glass, whenever it had happened. In whichever violent demonstration or burn zone cleansing it had been done. I don't know what possessed me to do it but I reached through, tossed the block aside and picked up the tattered pages, barely held together as they were. I recognised the text and my heart skipped a beat. George Orwell. 1984.

I looked up and down the now deserted and long destroyed street. Bloomsbury was barely recognisable in comparison to how I had first seen it. The remnants of twenty-two years of rioting and increasingly violent control, husks of burned cars still littering the pavements where they had been repeatedly ploughed by armoured police vehicles in the early days of the changes. When people realised what was happening and tried to stop it. Too late. Too little was done, too late for anything to work. I had once thought all of this would happen. Once called the whole situation Orwellian. I had however, like many others, not said it too loudly nor done anything about it. I'm as guilty as the architects of this.

I'd forgotten the feel of a book, paper being as rare as it now is, and found myself squeezing those tattered pages a bit too tightly. I could feel my finger tips digging in but couldn't let go, couldn't ease up. A fifty-four year old copper stood in a burn zone with a gun in one hand and less than half a book in the other. It felt like the very last piece of the past, the last tangible thing. The only anchor I could grasp at. The circling vulture squawked in delight as my soul blackened a further shade.

Despite the fact it had been twenty-two years, I had an overwhelming urge to smoke a cigarette. Of course they were rarer than paper, as rare in fact as rocking horse shit, but the craving was strong. Intense. I holstered the gun and, with the grunt of an old and weary man, sat down on the broken glass and began to read by firelight.

***

Crying, I tossed the tattered pages into the dying embers which had once been Tom and took my pistol from its holster, then placed it under my chin. Pulled the trigger. I had done nothing when I could have. I hadn't taken a stand. My chance to provide a solution had died and, with it, any chance of my own redemption. My last thought a sour 'at least'. No comfort.

At least I would no longer be part of the problem.

13th October 2014:

"Officer, please can you clarify your answer?" The Coroner peered over the top of her glasses, an attractive, raven haired woman. The bright, low, Autumn sun beamed through the window, reflecting off the face of her dainty Rolex. A small bar of light bounced around the ceiling as she gesticulated softly, creating a hypnotic effect. In the inquest chamber, a recently completed annex, all was silent aside from the odd shuffle of fabric as people shifted in their seats.

"Ma'am," a weak voice, one which sounded like it was coming from another person entirely, squeaked out into the room, a quality to it of being broadcast through golden syrup. The small bar of light moved from ceiling to wall and then disappeared as the Coroner sat forwards, clasping her slender hands together and resting them on top of the papers spread across her desk. The clerk to her left mirrored the forward movement, hand coming up, cradling his plump chin as he poised his pen. In that moment sirens thundered past, two sets, all attention was drawn momentarily to the bright scene outside. This fleeting distraction, lead somewhere else, two years before. Another October day.

***

The metal chair creaked as he sat down, not due to his size but just because the chairs at this place always creaked. He threw his rucksack between his legs, turned and knocked on the large glass window. The young Romanian waitress smiled at him, as she always did, and motioned she would bring his drink.

"So then big boy, what's new?" he asked, lighting a cigarette and stretching back, watching the world pass by on the pavement. I sipped my coffee, put the cup neatly back on the saucer and smiled.

"Well, I'm good. Work's as shit as ever. Getting more so by the minute but, generally, life is good." He smiled at this. "How's the discipline hearing looking?" For the briefest of seconds, a dark look crossed his face, literally a shadow, accompanied by a creasing of his forehead, then was gone. He drew deep on the cigarette and briefly let his eyes follow the path of a blonde woman as she passed by.

"I'm going to be out. Of that there is little doubt. But, they have agreed to leave the book." I watched him, to see if the shadow would his face once more. It didn't. He actually looked relieved. Serene even.

"That's bollocks but good at the same time," I said. He nodded slightly and blew smoke out of the corner of his mouth. "I just can't believe they are hoofing you out for telling the truth. And leaving the book alone...well, it just fucking confirms it."

He smiled as he replied. "In short my friend. The truth will out, and with it so shall he who finds it". The waitress brought his coffee with a smile and after a brief flirt she went back inside. He sipped it.

"You really are a whore," I said, laughing. He flicked his already smoked cigarette into the street, where it bounced off a moving taxi.

"I may be a whore. But very soon I will be a free whore, pimping myself wherever I see fit. Meanwhile you will drudge forward, ever more at the beck and call of your masters, chasing figures, hounding the innocent and turning a blind eye to the good and the great who can't keep their fingers out of the cookie jar or, in some cases, small children". I had to really hold the mouthful of coffee in, to avoid spraying it over a passing family.

"Very eloquent," I managed to regain my composure. "So, what next?".

"Well, I've been following up on the GPS stuff, you know the tagging I told you about. Really it's well beyond the usual grubby dealing but, I guess, now this is my full time job. So beyond grubby it is." He raised the tall glass of latte. I chinked my coffee cup against it.

"Cheers you bastard," I half growled and then joined him in appreciating the human traffic.

***

"Officer, are you with us?" The Coroner, was still leaning forwards but now looking less than amused.

"No ma'am." A less alien voice this time, more of the usual half growl. It was met by a scowl.

"Are you being flippant in my inquest?"

"No ma'am. The answer to your question is no ma'am." Even the clerk stopped writing and looked directly at me with an eyebrow raised.

"So in respect of the changes to your original statement you have nothing to say which may help this inquest?"

The lump in my throat tried to move, I held it, just and replied once more. Quietly and while staring at the floor. "No ma'am."

After I was dismissed from further questions, with some unguarded scalding, I made my way out, head down through the gaggle of journalists and photographers until I reached clear pavement. I'd held my breath almost the entire time, or felt like I had.

As I walked, shoulders slumped and staring at the floor, the phone rang in my pocket. I answered straight away. "Yes?"

"I saw. There were no issues with the school run today. Your wife and daughter are at home and it looks like they are having fun drawing in the kitchen."

The initial relief was replaced by panic, dropping like an ice-cold stone all the way through me. "I thought this was over now." I tried to keep my tone even, unimpressed, while my heart tried to leap straight out through my rib cage.

"People have long memories. You know that." He hung up, whoever the hell *He* was.

I stopped walking, looked up at the brilliant, bright sky and shouted at the top of my lungs. "Fuck."

*****

Looking back, what started him off was simple really. If I had known where it would lead I would have either stopped him or stood right with him. In my head I'd like to think the latter, but the drawn face in the mirror most mornings tells me it could have only been the former. At best. I've found a lot out, about myself, these last two years and I don't like much of it. And, all before that first phone call.

I remember it as clearly as my daughter's first word: "Your little girl looks pretty, her eyes are the same colour as your wife's. Change your statement, that's my advice. I'll be in touch."

My daughter's eyes are pale blue, just like my wife's. My daughter's first word was 'hat'.

***

He clumsily cracked the two pint glasses down on the table at the usual place. It was most irritating that it was always my bitter which sloshed out, while his lager remained intact. Full to the very top, without a single drop spilling.

In almost one movement he thudded back into the seat and raised his pint toward me. "Cheers you bastard." He didn't wait for me to raise mine, but gulped a quarter of it down like water, placed the glass back on the table and clapped me on the shoulder. "Not much minky in here tonight but, it is a school night."

"I'm surprised 'Mr Winky' hasn't dropped off," I said, pointing at his crotch and shaking my head, in what I hoped was comic reproach, as I spoke.

"Mr Winky will never drop off."

"No, but he may end up being cut off." I finally picked up my pint and sipped it, then sipped it again. Out of the corner of my eye I saw the 'look' come onto his face. I sipped a third time for good luck.

"Have you ever heard of biometrics?" I stared squarely at him. He had turned into his other self. His work self. The one which scared me more often than not.

"No. But then, you know I don't have an iPhone either." Absently I patted my pocket, where the indestructible Nokia sat against my leg.

"It's used by that company the chiefs went into partnership with, to help collate the mugshots and pass them around. Like the F.B.I. do in the U.S." I vaguely remembered something about this on the intranet and nodded, bade him continue. "Well kimosabe, they just teamed up with a group that represents retailers."

"Fascinating," I said and yawned as he paused to gulp more lager.

"I just found out something that's really dodgy about the whole arrangement."

"No surprise there then," I growled.

"Actually it is." He gulped again, knowing he hadn't had to say it while his eyes wandered over to the Hungarian barmaid. She flashed a smile at him which he returned, for once only half-heartedly. I waited, the benefit of friendship telling me he would continue without prompting. "You see, the chiefs are now selling off a load of nicks and we'll be having desks and offices in the supermarkets, right?"

"I'd like some burgers oh and by the way, I've been assaulted." He nodded furiously at this. "So what is the problem?"

"On the face of it, nothing. I mean think about it, coppers in the supermarkets might prevent a large amount of shoplifting." This time he paused, awaiting a response. He had a habit of getting cat and mousey.

"Sounds like a good thing then," I sipped my bitter and waited for him to hit me with it.

"Wrong." He paused deliberately for impact this time. "The facial recognition people are financially partnered up with the retail crime reduction group." He spread his hands, a non verbal *Ta-Dah!* I stared at him. Blankly. "Oh for fuck's sake. The retailers buy into facial recognition by paying an annual membership fee. The face people buy into the police chiefs via their own partnership."

"What are you getting at?" I was smiling as I knew. He knew I knew but, like a kid, he needed his big finish.

"I'm saying that the supermarkets just bought the police, to protect their losses of bacon and nappies and cheese." He sat back, looking self-satisfied and finished the last third of his drink, slamming the glass down on the table. "Now drink up you wet lettuce, mine's a pint."

***

I put my head down and picked up my pace, desperate to get away. As far away from the Coroner's Court as I could, the words of the last phone call still ringing in my ears. I wanted to be home, to be in the kitchen with my wife and daughter. I wanted to be the one watching over them, not the voice on the phone. As the chiefs had once been bought by the retailers, I had now been bought. The currency of the transaction was fear.

More sirens in the distance. Something was happening.

***

My wife kissed me quickly as I hurriedly moved the sandwich from my mouth, then jammed it straight back in again, freeing my hand to slide its arm into my jacket.

"You be safe out there," she said, smiling and hugging me again as I shrugged the rucksack onto my shoulders.

"Kiss the monster for me when she wakes up and I'll see you at some point in the morning love." I was chewing and showered her with crumbs. She pulled her 'yuck' face, perfected over ten years with me.

"Make sure you eat again later," she said, squeezing my bum and giggling as I opened the front door. I almost launched myself out, in a half jump.

"I love you." I kissed her on the doorstep,

then half jogged down the path to the street. She watched me for a while and I turned to wave again. She waved back and closed the door with a clunk, the brass knocker rattling slightly in the eerily silent evening.

I'd been there, at home, for about two hours and the sun had gone down when the call came. By then the raw, crippling panic, which had gripped my earlier journey, had subsided. Alleviated by the warmth, love and smiles of my small family. Even the feeling of being watched had tapered into a general uneasiness, but the weight of the phone in my pocket remained heavier than it had ever felt before. A traitor kept close. This new phone call was different, it came on the land-line; a rarely used item these days. It was work. It was happening again. The building sirens of the day made sense and my instincts had been correct. Something was happening. I - and just about everyone else – had been called in.

I remembered the London riots of 2011 only too well, sitting at home, watching them unfold on the news channels and calling work myself, to ask where they needed me. Now things were different in that respect. Since the Leveson bill on media restrictions had been passed - and since the BBC and ITV had found themselves stripped out for misbehaviour against the government - real time media had all but been curtailed. Nothing was broadcast until at least twenty-four hours after the fact. Every story had to go through a triple legal assessment before it was seen beyond the news room or in the columns of the three remaining newspapers.

Of course this was well embedded by the time the violent austerity protests of 2013 had taken place in every major town and city. The police response had been harsher than previously imagined and the clashes which turned violent on the morning of the 1st July had been subdued by the same evening. The streets had been a mess of soaking wet and bloodied protesters who had gathered for a one day strike - the last before the Industrial Action Bill came into force, permanently removing the right to strike. Almost exclusively every person involved had been a union member and the following day their attendee lists were seized remotely from computers and servers up and down Britain. The arrests began that evening.

What was happening tonight I didn't know yet, but the feeling of trepidation which had sat like lead in the pit of my stomach twice before was with me once again.

***

The bricks began to smash into the side of the riot van before it even stopped, broadside to the mass of people barricading the street only twenty-five metres away. We had lost our escort as it was diverted to another location en route and we were running short. Just an Inspector and four of us, as others struggled to make their way into the capital. Not that there were many to begin with after the cuts.

"We're wrong side on." I shouted from the back of the van, handing shields from the racks near the back doors to my colleagues. The thunder of thumping bricks and the roar of the crowd was deafening.

"What are you talking about?" the young Inspector shouted back. He had only been in the role a few weeks, having passed the earlier work based assessments of his Graduate Entry Programme within the first eighteen months. He looked at me as if I were a piece of shit on the bottom of his shoe and slid the side door fully open to face the crowd.

The petrol bomb hit him square in the face and he, and the interior of the van, were engulfed in a ball of flames.

"Out, Out, Out!" I shouted, slamming the back doors open. The smoke and flames in the confined space was already overpowering. I could smell my own burnt nostril hair. Bricks pelted the open door and it swayed on its hinges.

Covering my face with my arm, I moved back towards the flames, reaching and grabbing the first limb I could find that wasn't alight. I hauled it backwards fast and hard. The shell-shocked girl, who I had never seen before tonight, launched herself past me, straight out from the small cocoon of the open doors and into the road. She made it about five metres before a whole brick hit her in the top of the head and staved in her skull. She collapsed and lay there, body twitching spasmodically, even as it was pelted with more and more debris.

The fire at my back was now unbearable, even in the flame-proof overalls. I stood in the small, double-doored cocoon, yanked my helmet down onto my head, hoisted the shield on my right arm, facing the direction of the crowd, and ran in a straight line, hopping over the body of the dead police officer. I kept running until I reached a recessed shop doorway.

Panting I peeked out and saw a crowd of hundreds. They were starting to advance, cheering and laughing. If I stayed here I would be dead. I looked back to the flaming van and saw the driver, on fire, struggling out of the door. I saw the nearest junction, the way we had come, around one hundred metres away. We had seen other groups of police units only minutes before.

The fuel tank of the police van finally exploded, causing the advancing crowd to flinch backwards and whoop in delight. I took three deep breaths, exhaled hard and bolted.

***

The further I sprinted, the lower the level of ambient noise became, replaced by the overwhelming surround-sound of shouting, screaming and explosions. I sprinted around left-hand corner, only a street away now from where the other police units had been.

Not much further. The shield on my right arm had become a dead weight.

The car hit me and everything went black.

***

"The foundations of the state began to be laid with the concept of a 'Big Society', hailed as a way to transcend religious and class division. It was designed to provide a feeling of everyone being in this together." The stage suited him. The flamboyant, intense, bloke I had known for years had finally found a home.

The auditorium was full, a mixture of students, academics, coppers and the curious. The spring sunshine streamed in from outside and he paced as he spoke, the nervous energy I had always known on full display.

"In the first few years, the civil service and public sectors were brought in line with the goals of the Government - albeit that, by strict political definition, they were radicals, driving what they called free market liberation. Political opponents were carefully either absorbed into the coalition and kept in line or, subjected to intimidation by ongoing leaks to the largely right-wing media." He paused to make direct eye contact with a couple of the correspondents sat in the front rows, then continued with a mischievous smile. "This was followed by changes in legislation, quietly at first. A freedom bill, which subtly changed harassment - opening it up to include those who criticised ministers or other officials via social media. All the while measures were introduced to bring local, political control to the police and justice system. The army became an increasingly regular sight on home soil and voting boundaries were changed. Redrawn to address inequities in the 'more difficult to win' north and Wales."

I caught his eye and he held it for long enough to tell me he had been drinking. He was always on top form with one or two pints. Beyond that he got darker. This was one or two pints. He worried me but, by God, I was proud of him.

He left the police and his book exploded over the winter. We hadn't been in touch as often but I'd watched him, his increasing appearances on the television since being 'freed' as he called it. When I received the invitation to this university event there was no way I could miss it. I just wasn't sure they knew what they had let themselves in for. By the looks on faces across the room it seemed most of them had fallen foul of his mojo.

"The government made moves towards the restriction and abolition of unions and the Chancellor directly acted on the exchange of employment rights for compulsory contributions to pensions and a scheme of shares as a substitute. Those of lower income or unemployment were stripped of benefits from the state, always under the guise of the inherited debts of the nation from the previous socialist regime. Even the disabled were subjected to ongoing checks to have the level of their ability to contribute to the Big Society assessed. Returns to work became enforced, with many used to fill temporary posts without pay in order to continue to receive any kind of funds from the state. All were eventually priced out of the housing markets." He stopped, looked down, looked around, looked anywhere but at anyone.

Across the room I saw people leaning close to whisper. I heard one, saying he'd lost his place, muttering about the curse of inexperience. I knew exactly what he was doing though, and when the silence had drawn out long enough to be uncomfortable he exploded back to life, his voice booming out with a gleeful solemnity.

"This could be now. This could be next year. It certainly is a fair reflection, of the reforms and actions, of the current Conservative Government." He paused just long enough to look across the crowd, seeming to make eye contact with every single person present. "It could be Nazi Germany, circa 1933."

I was stunned. The room recoiled in horror, a physical leaning back by almost everyone there. There were several sharp intakes of breath.

***

I came to on the floor, gasping. The shield was trapped underneath me and the helmet felt claustrophobic but I could not feel much pain exploding anywhere - the new public order armour was pretty robust. I rolled onto my back. My breathing was still heavy from the running. I couldn't have been out too long.

I risked it and sat up, still no major pain but I was a mess of adrenaline. I could feel it building in my muscles again, in nervous bundles. I'd feel nothing until tomorrow. At least. I shook my head, pushed up the visor and then pushed cautiously to my feet. Everything seemed to be working. A few fireworks in my eyes, but even they subsided after a few seconds. I wobbled, then felt okay. That's when I saw the car. A Mercedes, with police markings. A command vehicle.

It sat idling at the junction. In the rear view mirror I could see the eyes of the driver, staring widely at me. I could also make out the silhouette of a passenger. A Merc meant it was a Commander.

I started towards the rear of the vehicle and as I did, the reverse lights came on.

***

As the Mercedes' gearbox whined and the broken bumper dragged across the floor, it mounted the pavement. Even though I was dazed, it seemed clear I wasn't going to be offered a lift.

All sense of fuzziness left me as the freshly built adrenaline exploded and I ran, not my best effort but running nonetheless, tight to the line of shop fronts. The Merc missed me by about three feet, reversing straight into the front of a franchised coffee shop, the flimsy metal-net shuttering bending inwards then breaking, tearing into new shapes and closing itself tight around the doors of the car as it came to a stop. The rear wheels had bumped up and over the shop frontage and were no longer on the floor. The sign, advertising the 'pop up police station' on Mondays and Thursdays, swung. A lump of broken glass, held together by printed adhesive sheet. I watched as it finally stretched and dropped onto the roof of the car with a clatter.

Even so, the driver was revving the engine, wheels spinning without traction as the car sat there. The passenger door repeatedly opened and closed against the twisted shuttering, never creating a gap of more than two inches. After a minute of fruitless attempts to drive forwards the engine cut out and the driver started the same pointless process of trying to open their door, which was also wedged shut.

To say I was not happy would have been a gross understatement.

I carefully approached the vehicle, passenger side naturally facing me. There was no way I was going in front of it again, having already been used to test the impact protection of the front bumper. Inside the car there was clear shouting going on. A lot of gesticulating. As I approached, the efforts to open the doors redoubled.

Through the windscreen I could see one of the four area commanders, Pemberton his name. One of the new breed. The passenger was even more curious, it was the Deputy Mayor for Policing and Crime. They both stared at me, their own argument temporarily forgotten. I'm not surprised, they had just tried to run me over a second time, deliberately, after all. That's when I heard the roar of shouting voices, rounding the corner. At which point it stopped briefly.

The crowd bunched up, staring at the police vehicle protruding from the window. At me, in riot gear, on my own. Flames flashed as petrol bombs were lit and then sailed through the air.

The first fell short, the second, third and forth hit the Mercedes on the protruding bonnet. I staggered backwards. The horrified faces behind the windscreen disappeared in a blanket of flames.

There was nothing I could do. Nothing. The crowd roared from behind the fireball, temporarily obscured. Two more petrol bombs landed. Using the flames as cover, I kept close to the shop fronts and ran for my life.

POVERTY

Without hope, there is no aspiration. Without aspiration, all that remains is acceptance.

This is a simple statement and one which may seem stark, even bleak, and somewhat depressing. Yet it is both a necessary statement and an accurate one. Even now I can remember the front room of the terraced, Victorian house, the putrid smell of rot, acrid sweat and dirt. Stacked food waste, rotting in plastic bags full of stinking condensation. The otherwise bare room - plaster falling in wet clumps from the walls and floorboards rotting under foot, constantly wet by the seeping compost from the black sacks – featured only two additional things: several piles of dog excrement, varying from fossil-dry to fresh, wet, and stench-creating, and a small child's doll, lying between two piles of filth.

In the hallway, the doll's face still staring up at me, caught in my peripheral vision, the stairs presented themselves as a slide. The carpet long detached from the steps. A lethal climb for an adult, let alone for a child – three of whom lived in the house.

This is poverty.

This is not the third world, not our common understanding of what poverty is: a far removed and distant problem.

This is poverty and it exists on our doorstep. In our towns. Our cities.

I don't know why we should find it so hard to accept this. Possibly it is the fear of recognising we just haven't looked too hard. Perhaps it is even the personal risks associated with acknowledging it is real and we must have, surely, known something of it being so but chose to blinker ourselves. Maybe we should look more closely, not at the statistical information coming to us daily - as a society subject to constant, numerical bombardment, we have largely become immune, cynical to it – but at what we see around us. Just around the corner. Or even next door.

If we do so, we might see the shambling woman in the dying seaside town, pacing and shaking, holed and threadbare clothing stained at the seat of the pants by clearly visible excrement. Should we listen, beyond the taunting shouts of the feral teenagers, their expletives, we might hear her mumbled reply: "Once you are down, you stay down...you'll see. One day you'll see."

Poverty exists and it is right under our noses, yet often we turn them up, seeing only what our self-preserving minds allow us to. *How could they let themselves get into that state?*

We ought to stop. We should stop. We must stop reacting in this fashion, because a whole generation of children is about to be tipped into such an existence. Into poverty. As a society, as people, are we even prepared to risk one child having to live like this, due our immunity to statistics? Simply put, it could be that two hundred thousand more children face this as their life. Conversely it could be that only one child, only five children, only ten, could be facing the front room. The empty belly and hollow, helpless, uncomprehending eyes which accompany it. Regardless of how many it effects, we should not be prepared to accept that any child has to be born, grown, and taught of life in this way. No child should be birthed down and stay down.

No child should have to see the doll's head staring back at them.

To grow up in such a way, never knowing any different, never feeling anything can change, is simply to grow without knowledge of hope. Of being able to dream of a different day. Because there is no hope, no dream – because time is preoccupied simply with surviving – then there can be no aspiration, no drive to change, only to survive. Or, if the learning is extensive enough, the pattern of learned helplessness will prevail. This latter is, in essence, the surrender to a situation, if you repeatedly try to escape it and are constantly hurt by the consequence of doing so. The double bind of not knowing hope and learned helplessness inevitably sees either the death of aspiration or ensures it was never a known concept to begin with. All that remains is acceptance and with acceptance of a lot, comes a simple fact: once you are down, you stay down.

Poverty exists, up close and personal, and our first step towards dealing with it has to be accepting this as fact. Once we do so, we can begin to make sure no child has to live their life in the unacceptable state of acceptance.

Poverty may not be visible on the street - not unless you are prepared to turn your nose down against your human instincts and acknowledge your fears, inviting the personal risk of doing so – but those rotting rooms may sit safely behind closed doors. Only we can provide hope, and only if we choose to do so.

Beyond the bedroom door, the dead girl lay among the refuse sacks. She was six.

CHEMICAL SAUSAGE

Personal Journal of Jack Rebbick

11th December:

It's cold. The clear, blue cold of December and the low sun shines down on the city.

From a late teens floor of the Greater London Police building, rented under a public finance initiative, I'm looking out at our capital in its golden haze: a landscape of grey, red and brown stone, punctuated by the fingers reaching for the cleaner, bluer sky - the BT tower, the shard.

The London Eye catches my attention, the giant wheel making me think of Alexander Pope. *Who breaks a butterfly upon a wheel?* The thought swirls around. The effort being put into dealing with me, the eye symbolic of London. Am I the butterfly? It passes and the lead-weight feeling returns to my limbs, the vague fuzz of adrenaline release again takes primacy and Pope dilutes like winter chimney-smoke, before being carried away on the bitter breeze.

I hope nobody else ever has to ask themselves: how have I been let down so badly by an organisation designed to uphold the law, fundamental rights, and the standards of a decent society?

I have had to ask this question and I can say, without doubt or shame, there is little in the dictionary - expansive as it is - which can adequately describe how I currently feel. That is, of course, emotionally. The physical manifestations of this experience are quite easy to list: my limbs alternate between feeling like immovable, lead weights and feather light entities, existing in some parallel reality and only just within my control. My heart rate varies between a slow, misfiring rhythm and rabbit-fast palpitations. My right eye twitches involuntarily and both are under-hung by dark, growing bags. I can't focus - my concentration swinging from full to a dysfunctional none at all. Frequently I shut down, like my son's robot dog once the batteries have gone. My temperature fluctuates uncontrollably between hot and cold; a pressure headache sits on my left temple; my glands are swollen; my throat's sore and my gums bleed at will. I have had the uncontrollable shakes, twice.

Emotionally? Emotionally. How to begin to describe the turmoil which is manifesting itself physically? A circular cycle is in full flow, a swing-o-meter which rushes from soul-wrenching dread to soul-sucking despair, to infuriating disbelief. There is also the lifeless, unresponsive, nothingness where, in the confusion, my brain just switches everything off - the most basic of human defence mechanisms. I am tired, worn out, exhausted. This has been brought about by what's happened, by what's been done to me. And for what? *For what?* This tiny, two word question is fundamentally one of the broadest, the biggest, the most enormous which could ever be asked. As I sit here, I have little else to do but answer it. No further comfort certainly - not even in the fact I remain a dedicated servant of the Crown and the Public.

My neck and cheeks are at the itchy stage of beard growth - I could shave of course, but so far I have promised myself not to. One day of growth for every day of this final, torrid mess.

Catching all of these thoughts, releasing them from the inner prison, is how the process of creating order where there currently is none is to start.

The face of the Detective Superintendent, has just confirmed the conversation I overheard half an hour ago; the blessing of an open plan office.

"Yes..." his words carried the ten feet to me as he spoke with the Detective Inspector at the Professional Standards Department. A pause then, as he listened to the voice in the telephone. "So all the social media and stuff...." Another, longer pause. "Yes. Thanks." His face, as he left for a 'meeting' two floors above, a combination of guilt, discomfort and poor you. The face of a police officer delivering a death message, or some otherwise bad news. I sat and sighed loudly.

Still, as he passed my desk I explained to him my feeling of dubiousness just before lunch, as an unfamiliar face had plonked fifty pence on my desk and said they'd found it outside the door. To me it smelt like an old-school honesty test. "Because of the current situation this makes me uncomfortable. At four o'clock I'll take it to reception as lost property, as there are no books for lost property that I can use."

He mulled this over and replied. "I can see why you're suspicious in your present situation," then bustled out to his meeting.

With PSD maybe?

My heart fluttered then sank.

The London Eye, the wheel, is still there staring at me. Briefly I stare back. The realisation, long awake, resurfaces again: whatever happens, the PSD will press ahead with some form of discipline. Regardless of the hash they've made so far, they will go for second and third bites of the cherry. In the courts of justice this wouldn't wash but in the courts of kangaroos they can - and will - do as they please. Behind closed doors, unchecked and uncontrolled, they will act out their fancies and fetishes.

I reach for my phone, to send an email to my solicitor, but my lead, dead-weight hand drops as soon as it is raised. So far they have received no reply from PSD, as they are still 'considering' their reply. All the while the wheel spins slowly, waiting, watching me from the corner of my eye. Silently.

Ironically this all revolves around silence. The art of silent dealings, the enforcement of silence. In all my noise I was right: in the end, it is the more powerful weapon. I said this myself some months ago, I boldly begged for silence to send a strong message.

But what a good, brave silence that was. Around me now, swallowing me, another silence - a doomed silence. A hungry, greedy, violent silence, which is suddenly broken.

The Detective Inspector, the Detective Chief Inspector - siblings no less - and the Sergeant burst into the office. I tense up, adrenaline bursts. They have brought the two efficiency experts from the Home Office. Standing behind me they talk and talk in what can only be described as Orwellian duckspeak. I can't talk back to them, not so much even acknowledge them. My discomfort increases. I freeze - shoulders and neck tense, staring straight ahead. They remain, talking. I can't even say hello. The Sergeant leads them out and only then do I finally exhale, slumping in my seat. The pen trembles in my hand and a momentary urge to vomit overcomes me.

"Are you writing War And Peace?" asks the Detective Inspector, hovering over my shoulder, peering down at the paper he has no business reading. His frantic mannerism bothersome, creepy, sickening.

I mumble "no," and shuffle the papers away so he can't see them. Can't capture my private thoughts. He floats away, only to be replaced by the Sergeant, my allocated welfare officer, who presents me with a large carrot, cut in two.

"Look at the size of that, too big for my lunch box."

The sense of absolute despair grabs me by the throat and shakes me like a rag doll. A shiver passes up my spine, coccyx to nape. My head shimmers slightly and with that comes more adrenaline. This constant up and down of chemicals will shortly bring about a collapse. Of this I have no doubt. Even my body, which I widely regard and treat as indestructible - which has proven itself so repeatedly - will not deal with this indefinitely. A crash will come but, as the DI and Sergeant both now begin to hover at my shoulders to try and see what I am writing, more adrenaline dumps itself into my blood. My senses feel alive, my vision clear; limbs on their way from lead weight to feather light. I glance up and for a moment the wheel doesn't scare me.

Some brief 'taskings' take little time. A three year, risk based analysis of burglary as a whole. Simple, although annoying such analysis must be redone repeatedly, or the interpretation expanded, until the result suits the needs of the academic studies of the Detective Chief Inspector.

I complete it properly, adding layers of further information which are then ignored. I sigh again but have come to expect little more. Then: re-running a weekly assessment of burglary using mapping software, this time including data which was not deemed of use the week before. Always a re-run, an afterthought or an ulterior motive.

Outside, the descent of the sun. Running fast, a mad downhill dash on the western horizon. The waters of the Thames, warm in comparison to the freezing city outside at least, slowly start to shroud London in mist and the awful wheel disappears, out of sight until tomorrow. The BT Tower, not on the river, stands as a red-lit candle, baseless in the gathering darkness. Closer, the grey, brown and red stone of the landscape fades to an eerie arc-sodium glow of faint orange. Green and blue twinkles around car-parks and estates, a blanket of earthbound stars below while those overhead are still obscured, hidden. They wait, to later mirror what's underneath them in the creeping mist.

The hopeless feeling returns in a wave and in the bathroom I calm myself. The Sergeant, my welfare officer, asks me a question right there at the urinals: "Have you heard anything from PSD?"

"No, have you?"

"No."

Later a box will be ticked, boldly stating my welfare has been looked after, that I am A-okay. All the while the Thames' mist creeps westward, southward. Faint twinkles appear along the river as the towering office blocks light themselves, a sea of Christmas illuminations - the Shard a slim tree, barely visible.

My eyes feel heavy, drained of the will to stay open. I've heard nothing for yet another day, aside that which I overheard. To the left of the computer screen, empty coffee cups, seven in total, and yet one more still full, hot and satisfying. To the right sits the suspect fifty pence. The thought of touching it makes me feel ill, tainted. I will leave it there. My whole body screams. I can't. If a cleaner takes it overnight the blame will lie with me. My reduction to such turmoil over a fifty-pence piece is one of the most upsetting and telling aspects of the day. In a simple piece of currency I have wrapped up the emotional mess into which I am being forced. You see, the PSD largely relies upon this, especially in cases such as mine. My eyes get heavier still and my neck is beginning to stiffen solid through tension.

Outside of the windows full dark races onwards and to the right of the BT Tower I catch sight of what looks like a further wheel, glowing in a white arc. I'm unsure if it is City Hall but fix on the idea it is, just to avoid the thought of a night wheel - a compliment to that which stared at me so coldly earlier. The group of stripes, pips and crowns leave, a small clique of sixth formers making their way home and, once their uncomfortable wake has subsided, my heart starts to lift. Soon: the journey. Soon the three hour trip home, the tube, the train, the bus; the cold of the East.

The mirror in the locker room shows me a ghost. A hollow-eyed shell, in transformation from phantom in uniform, to phantom in jeans and a Puffa jacket. My torn rucksack, which I can't afford to replace, slung heavy on my shoulder, the increasing weight of paper becoming the load of my life. The silent figures in the lift don't even grunt greetings as we descend. I lose myself in this paper and one happy memory of the day from the opposite end of it: a tap on the shoulder, a conspirational whisper.

"I follow you on social media. I can't believe what they are doing."

I shuffle the weight on my back and walk out, into the grounded constellations of London. Into the underground. Two stops cancelled on the Central Line - one for illness, one for fire. None on the tube express any concern for anyone else. It seems, down in the tunnels much as in my tower, the self is at the centre of the universe. I glance up and down the carriage, no friendly faces - but that's not what I am seeking. I am looking for familiar faces.

The fifty-pence piece is the simple explanation: am I being tested? The complexity is: am I being followed? Earlier I saw a familiar face, at least I thought it was - from the night before, sat at the pub and sharing a half a table. "Do you mind if I sit here?" it had asked.

I had shrugged.

This situation is getting to me, but not

without reason. The PSD are well known for inventive practices, so I look again, to see the familiar face which will tell me all. I see none and read a little Raymond Carver.

At the bustling train station a quick cigarette in the cold night air and then the train. No seat but a damp patch of rough carpet, like a wall-to-wall doormat - my left side propped to the door and a cool wind blowing onto my already numb buttocks. My feet are pressed against one bulkhead, my back to the other, knees bent. I start to get pins and needles after the first twenty minutes. From the rucksack I slide the photocopies of articles on whistleblowers, brought to me by a Chief Superintendent, the one person who - in the tower at least - has genuinely asked if I am okay. I will take him up on his offer of coffee tomorrow.

As my thoughts barrel along so does the train, homeward-bound in the dark, away from the tower, from the wheel, from the grounded blanket of stars. Slowly the tension begins to subside. Within my emails, a retired Assistant Chief Constable confirms everything I've said about the culture of policing, police leadership, figures. He shares my passion, my morals and my despair.

The train speeds up and the draft creeps under my jumper to the base of my spine. My right kidney complains but I just cannot move - buttocks numb, pins and needles spreading outwards from the balls of both feet. I close my eyes briefly and slow my breathing, in that second recapping my day - rediscovering those in the office know more about the investigation into me than myself or my lawyer. Rediscovering that phone calls are taking place and decisions being made. Rediscovery the road is not yet travelled but the destination is known.

I close my eyes once more, taking another, slower set of breaths, calming myself as a passing train slams through the night, jolting the door as air streams smash into one another and become a displaced storm. In the darkness of closed eyes I see London's lights twinkling at me, the fearsome coin on the desk. The adrenaline is fading now and tonight I will crash, sleep four or five hours and do it all again.

Behind closed eyelids, I summarise the day, the last few weeks. I silently mouth the words "it stinks, it leaks, it lies and now it will invent". And there they are, my thoughts externalised. My whole body shudders in the relief. The stars look down, as they should and the day is finally set right.

I have now been trapped in my own life for twelve days and, in the final, dark walk of the last yards, the depth of the situation hits me. Like Alcatraz all those years ago, the principle which makes restricted activity so effective is the maddening nature of it. On the island, prisoners could hear the city, see the city, the sound-waves carrying voices across the bay. Sat in the office, in a world I am no longer fully part of, I am on the island - no better example than earlier, when the Home Office chaps were there and I stared rigidly ahead as they spoke directly behind my shoulders. The penny, or the fifty-pence if you prefer, finally dropped: the misconduct process is designed to force a surrender, either to make it stop or to drive you off with stress or a nervous breakdown. Probably so performance and attendance regulations can do the work where misconduct fails.

12th December:

The frozen night stretches out as it does in winter, encroaching on the day. As I step out of the back door the air bites at my ears and fingertips. The cigarette crackles every time I draw on it. Overhead the stars are a clear blanket of shining pin points. Orion, drawing his bow, stands proud, his belt glittering. The ever watchful hunter.

On the train, hurtling toward the city, the dark horizon begins to pale, shifting from darkest black to a washed-out, dark blue. Soon the sun will break its shackles and race upwards to its low winter seat. And, as the rails are eaten by the locomotive, so is the distance between me and whatever the day will bring.

I am calm, heartbeat steady, belly empty. Food holds little importance or interest at present. For now I hurtle onwards, towards fate. An unstoppable force with the city and its wheel the immovable object. What a frivolous thought, a product of the morning imagination, alive and well in my soul. Will today bring any news, any result? Anything. I believe at this moment that it may, yes. My heavy eyes convince me so as they glance out of the window and see stations slip by, ghostly and dim-lit as they sail past in pockets of mist. Externally, the silent world shows parts of itself while, in front of me, the young bankers reek of stale alcohol and discuss the women they have fucked and will fuck. Their world one of money, parties, booze and sex. That lot is theirs and one I wish I had pursued, if only I could ever resolve the selfish side of me would take full control.

As these thoughts wisp away, gladly released, the dark blue sky becomes paler still and the shroud of mist grows, the city and the day ahead as yet equally unclear. Passing Stratford, passing Bethnal Green, London looms out of the murk. Old and new sits side by side and equally grotty before we disappear, creeping slowly into the bowels of the station. The blue-grey sky replaced by metal and concrete, and below a spaghetti of littered tracks.

The white platform and bright lights take over - I have arrived in the Accident and Emergency of commuting to the city; a bustling transport triage where, in the morning, home lives are discarded - extracted at the barriers, as hundreds are immunised against the day ahead.

Underground once more, no delays, stoppages or gawking. No familiar faces and, unusually, empty seats in all carriages. As the tower looms in the foggy, morning light, my limbs become heavy and my heart rate increases, becoming rabbit-fast once more.

In the bathroom I shave briefly, to tidy up the beard which has started to curl. In the locker room the ghost in jeans and a Puffa jacket becomes a ghost in uniform.

The Chief Super has emailed me the latest brain-wave from the think tank, which I had already read in any case. They suggest the creation of Citizen Police Academies. I reply, repeating my concerns, not only about the breadth of influence over ministers and GLP leadership, but also over the speed at which a stabbing can occur. The days of have-a-go heroes are finished and the reason for this is the glinting blade. However, what do I know about the practicalities of operational policing? I am but an uneducated, blue collar, police officer. If I sat in the safety of Westminster, maybe I would have a better handle on the streets.

To my amusement a private message arrives via social media, from the Professional Standards Lead - a great anomaly by name - of the National Police Union. He wishes me luck in 'this unfair process'. The irony doesn't escape me that even the lead knows how this works - how it is weighted - yet effectively melts, as the chocolate teapot does. I ask him, knowing the answer, what interception authority is required to obtain the content of private messages. His reply is even more chocolatey.

"Assume they can and will access and use. Legal arguments are for afterwards."

His initial message plays through my mind once more: "don't forget they will use anything from on here too." I sit and sigh heavily while smoking a cigarette and then return to the office.

The coffee machine whirs as the new Inspector, whose name I don't yet know, says "You know it's a discipline offence not to wear epaulettes on your fleece, but then you can't speak to anyone so how do I tell you?" The moment of light relief is most welcome, especially as I have had to bow out of the Christmas meal, losing my £10 deposit in order to meet my condition not to have contact with the public.

"One reply to that Sir," I say, before raising two fingers at him and blowing a raspberry.

He laughs. "That's two things."

"Consider it partnership working," I say and return to my desk, eight feet from the nearest human.

Outside the heavy shroud has finally lifted, revealing a grey horizon with blue sky above. Not even the spent candle of the BT Tower rises high enough to touch the crisp watercolour. Not even the Shard, the top of which I can just make out. My heart feels increasingly heavy and I can almost hear the sound of thread being pulled through the fabric of the stitch-up going on around me. For a moment I count church spires to distract me. Four. Four without really seeking.

Some brief Google searches from earlier prey on my mind, they make a good deal of sense. I'm now well versed in the psychology of learned helplessness and understand exactly how the police has landed itself in this mess, where thought and expression of anything but the norm result in so many shocks and noises they now wash over most, and all efforts to make it stop have been concluded, abandoned even.

Ironically, I receive an email asking for advice on wanted offender management. I send an extract from one of the models I wrote - the reason I was asked by one of the Chieftains to move here. I follow up with personal advice. "Please make sure the established (and commented on) GLP practice of listing suspects in the note pages doesn't take place."

This is done by many of the GLP command units at the behest of their leaders to stop true outstanding suspect figures from appearing on lists. I refer back to the latest question I posted on the corporate message board: I had asked what a Crime Assessment Policy was and how the GLP proposed to reduce the number of open investigations. Of course, the answer is clear. It is the formalisation, the legitimisation if you like, of the wholly misunderstood and constantly downplayed system of reducing crime by manipulating the figures, and by closing crimes swiftly to avoid any burdensome investigations or requirements for resource. This is the future, the learned helplessness phenomenon in full swing.

The message board of course goes on, with two more people raising the issue of manipulated statistics. This time the command centre are marking incidents with arrival times, even if no-one has attended. The target culture is quite well engrained and becoming more endemically corrupt as time passes. Further to this are the added pressures of targets within PSD for 'successful' performance and misconduct proceedings.

The environment is polluted, poisonous, cut throat. Like it or not, we are in a pressure cooker and very shortly it may explode.

Grey clouds mottle the sky and start to bring on early darkness. As it begins to happen I check up on the union website. No news on the Bill being discussed at second hearing in the Houses of Parliament - the one which will compel officers under investigation to answer questions when being interviewed. Placing them in a unique position in society, where even the most horrific of criminals have a right to silence. The world is becoming lop-sided and skewed, a never ending waterfall supported by those who claim to lead the service, having risen successfully by driving the performance culture.

The feeling of needing to vomit, after the earlier chocolate message, hasn't yet fully subsided and my solicitor still hasn't replied to an email. I note that my phone went askew while I was trying to send it and I had to set my emails up all over again: I can't help but wonder if my phone has been hacked. The cursed fifty-pence, now locked in the Sergeant's drawer, plays on my mind again but looking up I feel relieved to find the dreaded wheel, the London Eye, remains obscured in winter mist. One small blessing at least. One small blessing as the candle of the BT Tower is lit and a red sunset reflects off the glass walls of the tall City towers.

The one real announcement from the union, on the think tank report, sits on the website and then I see what alarms me the most. A shiver runs across my neck and my eyes widen briefly. They fully support the draft Communications Data Bill. The union, the same union which told me earlier, only hours before, PSD would view and use private messages, worrying about the legal aspects after the fact. The urge to vomit is almost overwhelming.

If the police cannot police themselves ethically and, as per the Lord Chief Justice, should only continue to police themselves without worry about bothersome legalities, then how on earth can they be trusted with new access to communications data? Abuse will pile on abuse, stinking and yet revelling in its own acutely self-aware repugnance. I hold down the sick which is desperately trying to escape, at the same time trying to cope with an overwhelming sense of panic and defeat. Of repulsion and horror.

The clouds begin to clump into a more solid sheet of grey and night begins unusually, on the horizon. The sun races westwards, hidden from view. In the lift, carrying very expensive pin-boards used to gather ideas in rooms filled with bullshit and ego, the Sergeant asks "Have you heard anything from PSD?" I look at him with hollow, tired eyes, from a bearded face, with clear discomfort written on it for all but an idiot to read.

"No," I say and in that second he makes a mental note to record that my daily welfare needs have been met. I sigh as we return, empty-handed, to the office. This is one big, farcical mess, a laughing beast. The clouds are gathering in the freezing wind.

13th December:

Cigarette smoke plumes from my mouth and nostrils in the cold night air of Liverpool Street station's entrance. It catches in the subtle wind and is dragged left, to the mousey blonde with the woollen hat. She doesn't appear to notice, but her scarf obscures all except her eyes. Plume after plume blows towards her from the small group of nicotine addicts: the police officer the banker, the PR girl, the tourists, and the beggar.

I turn my attentions back to Sir Robert Peel, sitting above Krystals off licence, directly sandwiched between Talking Heads, a hair salon on his left, and a pawnbrokers on his right. Above him, lifeless, dark windows are framed in a narrow building. The image strikes me as making a great deal of sense - the Chief Officers are pushing for cops in shops as part of their partnership arrangements with Retail Crime Prevention and, in Parliament, policing is a football subject to much talk from the left and a great big sell-off on the right. All the while those at the top of the service are soul-less windows, each as transparent to the darkness within them as they are dim, dull, and lacking redeeming inner glow. I've just read their latest, snivelling, grovelling press release, bemoaning the sale of their wonderful stately home of leadership. Many a tear will be shed as the beehives, paid through taxpayer's money, are passed on to new ownership. Reality bites, I guess.

Perhaps, had the policing equivalent of Hogwarts produced more who sting like bees, rather than those who flit from role to role like perverse, socialite butterflies, then maybe old Robert Peel wouldn't find himself at such a portentous crossroads. Of course, soon the butterflies will gather once more, present company excluded due to rights violations, to create a new and withering social media policy. The great irony being many have refused to attend because they find the corporacy so galling and, not only will it be led by one man who used social media to try and expose a high profile, anonymous account against his wishes, but also by another police leader who only replies if he likes what he is being told. I used to find his constant ignorance as to the existence of others fairly amusing. I now see it as a public expression of all which has led Robert to his crossroads and the service into learned helplessness.

I cast off the cigarette, having forgotten entirely about the mousey blonde - and the motley smokers - and head straight to the train, managing to procure a seat for the second time in eight months, my normal place being on the doormat carpet with a draft on my buttocks.

"I'm on a train, I'm on a train Scrappypie," says the blind man next to me, shouting into his phone. I wholeheartedly agree as I begin to hurtle through the dark and away from the city, my day turning over in my head, relived once again.

The alarm wakes me at seven, rather than the usual five, and the headache hits me on the brow as soon as my eyes open. I roll slowly out of the duvet, into my waiting flip-flops and quietly grab the laid out clothes, before noisily opening the bedroom door. In the cold dining room I switch on the heating and put on my lumberjack shirt, then stand at the back door smoking a cigarette while the kettle boils. There's no mist outside but only a few stars poke out from thin cloud. In the silence I can once again hear my cigarette crackling as I draw on it. The kettle chuckles and then clicks off so, as my toes go cold, I put the cigarette in the gutter, close the door with a shiver, and make instant coffee. It serves me well - to knock down the two ibuprofen - and provides the perfect place in which to dunk Italian breakfast biscuits from a German supermarket, which facilitates shopping on a modern British budget.

The DI has replied to my text of the night

before, telling him I am going to see the Doctor:
"Are you okay?"

I contemplate numerous profane responses and
in the end stick safely with none, drink another
coffee and start to get ready, being interrupted
pleasantly by my boy cuddling me, delighted to
see his dad and picture-perfect with his bed hair.
"Daddy! Don't you are working today?"

"Not yet," I tell him.

"I love you Daddy."

"I love you too, monkey."

We head back upstairs and put his dressing
gown on, then wake up his little sister. She rolls
over excitedly, smiles at me and shouts: "Makka
Pakka" and "In The Night Garden," pronounced
ah-kah, ah-kah *and* ih-ga-gah. *She giggles as I*
cuddle her, claps, then puts her dummy in her
mouth with a smack.

After breakfast it's the magic of Advent
Calendars. They both high-five me with their tiny
hands.

I finish getting ready and kiss my family before
heading into the bitter, bitter cold. The headache
has passed and I am leaving my home in daylight
for the first weekday in months, joining the long
queue at the surgery behind a woman with some

of the curliest hair I have ever seen. It's an hour and forty minutes before I am seen and, by this point, I am so engrossed in The Trial by Franz Kafka, I've forgotten where I am and why I am there. I saunter into room five and the Doctor looks at me curiously.

"So, tell me what's going on." She leaves it hanging for a second and I take a moment longer than is comfortable to reply. However, she is soon distracted as I reel off the situation. The physical impact and the emotional strain. She sits agog and agape.

"So, laugh or cry, that's where we are Doc."

For a second she appears hypnotised but then springs back to life and five minutes later I'm getting on the bus at the stop outside, her offers of drugs, which I declined, running through my head. Sleeping pills and anti-depressants. At the moment I just can't afford any dullness of my senses and would walk straight into the trap of being labelled ill *by those who would wish me harm. I accept the offer of a referral to counselling though. Talk is something purely requisite to all humans – an activity which humans have been genetically bred to do in order to ensure their survival. To talk, at present, is something I have been prevented from doing and it's with a sad, listless sense of irony I have now been prescribed it by my General Practitioner.*

Eventually I leave the sleepy village and its frosted slate roofs behind, and begin hurtling toward London, in the end making it to the office at half past one.

I find the thoughts of the morning are not preservable as the blind man records an Audioboo about a bag of crisps. The first giggles in the carriage start with "big East Anglian spuds" and the tears begin at "a very chemical sausage." A very chemical sausage indeed, and far from the first suspect thing I have heard today.

In the tower, in which I am imprisoned - a short haired, bearded Rapunzel, I transform from ghost to ghost and am met by my union rep. Slowly he is making progress, making representations and, without assistance from me, has arrived at the description of the situation as intolerable. *But these to and fro statements are more for him than me, to demonstrate - maybe even to himself - he is doing* something. *The greatest tell is when he sums it up without a prompt to do so.*

"I've documented the health and safety issues so, if you find yourself on a ledge somewhere, it lays with someone else." I don't hold it against him: blame culture has created this. Prolific at every

level of the service.

"Don't worry, I'm seeking external help and frankly am strong enough to never get onto a ledge." Of course, I won't be going off sick either, not now, because we both know how they use the performance and attendance regulations where discipline fails.

He stares at me for a moment, eyes moving quickly as he studies my face. I watch his decision, to let me in on something confidential, taking place without a single word being said. "They use it all the time now" he says, drumming the desk for emphasis and staring briefly around the open plan to see who is listening. "People with cancer, degenerative diseases, all forced out. It's horrendous and getting worse. All because so many play the system for their own benefit, to get something which suits them."

I am well versed in this, I've seen it, dealt with. Been a victim of it then and now.

"We all know it's happening." He says the last with resigned finality, we part company and I make way to my desk, where I sit uninterrupted for around ten minutes.

With that the DI bustles in, accompanied again by the two men from the Home Office.

"How was the Doctor? Are you okay? Anything I should know about?" he asks and I mutter no as my discomfort increases

Suddenly, the shorter civil servant is stood directly next to me, on my left. My heart is rabbit-fast once more.

"Hello! Nice to see you! How are you?" I stare dead ahead at the screen, painfully aware of the DI on my right and the other man behind me.

"I'm really sorry, I am not allowed to speak to you." Out of the corner of my eye I see the stunned look on his face. Behind me I hear a chuff, which sounded like the gasting of a flabber.

To my right the Detective Inspector flushes red. "Well I don't think it need be so rigorous...." He then tails off and becomes inanimate as the penny finally drops, the cursed fifty-pence which I had handed in at reception, is no longer my weight or torment. On his face I see it pass to him. The currency of dawning reality has suddenly become legal tender.

I push away from the desk in mortified embarrassment and, head down, walk around the dividing column at the centre of the open plan, disappearing out of sight to the far West end of the office. I go to brief the analyst I have arranged to meet but was not due to see until some time afterwards. When I return, the three, who had all been left open-mouthed, were gone. I email the DI immediately, expressing my concerned horror, then put my fleece on and go downstairs in the express lifts.

The monthly senior leaders gathering is taking place and I hit the lobby at a break, so it is flooded with brass and spaghetti. Outside the revolving doors I see a shock of short, Norwegian hair. It's a Commander who once kidnapped me after I presented some work on enhanced resourcing and intelligence briefings. They've always been interested and warm.

"Hello," I say and they stare at my sunken eyes and growing beard, then smile. They can't remember my first name.

"Hello, good to see you, how are you?"

"I've had better lives," I reply.

"What's the matter?"

"Have you seen last week's papers? Guardian, Times. Independent?"

"No," they say, but I see them already starting to think.

"Ah, well, I told some home truths and am now up for gross misconduct." Their face changes

completely, the smile gone like it was on a switch. They slow their pace and drop back behind me without a further word or desire to associate.

I sigh and hide myself, in a huddle of one, in the only nook of the smoking area. I don't even enjoy the two chain smoked cigarettes as I am too busy wondering at the fact I have become an unfortunate addition to the sole of a shoe. The change in their face and step will stay with me. That's how it happens, that's how lines are drawn. How a good intention becomes a chemical sausage - an unwanted and unexpected after taste. For me it is the way I am being treated, for them the fact they blessed me with a smile, crossing some unknown line in the sand. They feel tainted by association.

I must deal with the legal insurance and call them, to contest the reason my claim won't be paid as long as I use the solicitor I've elected. Google quickly provides my reasons: the solicitor they prefer works with the PSD. I draft the email, quoting their own conflict of interest policy and specifying clauses, before sending it to my brief for a critical eye. They later reply, describing it as excellent, so I send it. The only thing to do is await a response.

Darkness clamours across the city, holding it in a ghostly grip as it starts to twinkle with distorted light. The office becomes the deck of the Marie Celeste, emptying of all souls.

The DI and his brother, the DCI, pause at my desk.

"We've written to PSD to get the ridiculous conditions lifted," says one.

"We can't have a repeat of that, with the Home Office chaps," says the other.

"We'll get it sorted." They both say.

They leave.

In my mind I see Tweedle Dum and Dee getting in the lift, arriving in Wonderland carrying a giant fifty pence between them.

14th December:

For no reason I wake up in the dark, with the overwhelming feeling I have missed my alarm and overslept.

After a few seconds I gain enough wits to check on my phone, the bright numbers glowing at me. 03:35 burns into a white and red fuzz which remains for a good while even after my eyes are closed again. I lay there awake for an hour and twenty-five minutes then get up, switching off the alarm before it has chance to ring its Tibetan bell.

Over coffee I come to two literary conclusions and one personal one. The personal one is the most simplistic: I feel better. No rhyme, no reason, no anything. Just a sense of feeling more like me. More whole and more real.

I turn my attention to Raymond Carver and his book of short stories, *What do we talk about when we talk about love?* At the table, in my pyjamas, I intimately know two more things. Firstly, Carver's book is the exact equivalent of a blog. Secondly, I recognise each of the short stories was intended to be a book, an idea which poured out of him from a conversation had or overheard, and then spent its flame as it slipped elusively away. I myself have several of these on hard drives and USB sticks.

With that, Carver drifts off, being replaced by Kafka and his Trial. Having devoured it in two days, having also spent much of it wanting to slap some sense into the story and the protagonist, I conclude Kafka was writing about himself and the story is representative of a personal trial he put himself through over a woman who he represents as his neighbour. The last chapter is her leading him to a lonely place, where a knife is twisted in his heart. Until then I had toyed with the idea the charge against K. was rape - against his neighbour - and the secret court was little more than his own guilt ridden trips to brothels. A figment of a fractured mind driven into being by guilt.

With those thoughts completed and articulated I leave home quietly, arriving equally quietly in the office. My peace is disturbed by a moaner, who regales the Sergeant and I with a story of how he has bought the registered trademark for 'Complete Policing', the flagship GLP programme of the current chief, and intends to sell it back to the service for £20,000. We are poles apart he and I. So inane is his claptrap my mind wanders to the story from this morning's Metro, about the girl awarded £10,000 out of court by the GLP after they bungled an investigation of a serious sexual offence - of which she was the victim.

Her mother made an excellent point, with which I find no fault or inaccuracy: "They fought dirty defending this and had they put as much effort into the investigation, as they had defending their collective ego, we wouldn't have needed to be here." It rings true and apt. The GLP should be investigating the serious issues I have raised but have opted for me instead. The moaner is the exemplar of how this has happened: his trademark is worth ten thousand more than an abused victim of crime, because it benefits him.

The Sergeant stands to my left, the window behind him framing the grey, wet misery of London. A handful of snowflakes fly horizontally in the wind. He neither stops gluing cut out phrases to card, nor bemoaning his current activity.

"I'm a Sergeant with fourteen years service and my job is fucking Blue Peter." I glance at him. "In 2015 or whenever the hell the next promotions are, I'll sit in a board, with years of experience and they won't believe what I have done anyway. This is pointless, job satisfaction: zero."

He carries on gluing regardless, then leaves to be trained on the world's most basic mapping software. I finish my chicken sandwich, eat the plastic consistency pain-au-chocolat, and head downstairs. The rain seems to ignore me as I walk and I arrive unmolested at the rear of the building, not even the slightest glisten of moisture on my fleece.

On my way back inside a voice at my shoulders. It's a DI, based at the historic home of the GLP, a fully fledged member of the fast-track promotion scheme and genuinely nice bloke. The first and last time we met he asked, with some surprise, why I wasn't on the scheme myself. I raise half a smile and he firmly shakes my hand.

"I hope you are holding up, considering everything."

"I've had better weeks."

His wishes are warm as I step into the lift and he watches me go, a look of confusion and sympathy on his face. I was happy to see someone sincere and hope we can talk properly again in the future. On my desktop screen Glorious Leader himself makes statements about savings and officer redundancies under the police regulations, while a link underneath, on the same page, announces recruitment of new PCs under the new entrant scheme - requiring that people pay for a Police Qualified Learning Certificate. This double announcement causes a stir on the message board and, to me, reinforces previous rumblings the new recruits, at a starting salary of about £18,000, are referred to as 'twofers' by senior managers. Outsourcing, it seems, is also squarely on the menu.

In the outer world, the three people in the office - all derivatives of the letter M - are discussing rejected flexible working applications. They were offered a rough Monday to Friday with regular long weekends (for me a dream having spent eight years on shifts) but they are upset because they prefer shorter days and more days off, as they have previously been allowed. All three are now pontificating as to how the needs of their jobs can come before their personal needs.

"I'll sue them," says one.

"When will I see my children?" asks another.

They are joined by others and immediately head for tea as a group, to discuss collective action.

I once raised the issue of shift patterns, which affected thousands of GLP's response officers across London and, ultimately, meant one of the recent periods of civil unrest went on for days. In that, I went above and beyond. Sadly all I see here is self interest being applied without perspective or thought for others. Worse still, it was this very department, these very people, who supported and justified that which I had fought against with good cause. It's the irony of karma, I suppose.

At three o'clock I'm done, headed home to make it there for six or six-thirty, with my wife being off out to work at seven. Fatherhood, my true joy, supersedes every other aspect of my life. The cuddles and complaints of both my children is what warms my heart and cools my head at all times. I change from uniform to jeans and Puffa jacket and note that, at least today, I don't have the ghost like qualities which have haunted me as apparitions through the rest of the week. Although tired, the bags under my eyes feel and look less evident, my cheeks less pale. My eyes are more focused, bluer and less lifeless.

17th December:

The morning is dark but the air is not as cold as the crisp and frosty Siberian weather of the week just ended. Fresh in my mind is the family time, that precious period punctuated by the boy skinning his nose on a shoe rack in TK Maxx - the difference between the concerns of age and youth made clear in our responses. For me huge worry he had broken his nose rather than just scraped it; for him the concern was much simpler.

"Daddy, I'm upset because I think I probably can't go to the Kissmass party tomorrow."

The end result makes us both cheer up: it isn't broken and he will go to the party. The rest of the shopping passed without incident, the final, pre-Christmas expedition a success.

Today, however, brings an overwhelming stomach cramp, the thought of work manifested physically. I take deep breaths until it passes then make coffee and sit down at the table, the radiator behind me pinging a few times as the heating warms up.

In the news I find mention of a police officer arrested by Professional Standards. It appears they are one of the group who leaked the ministerial corruption allegations to the media. In the Guardian article my own case is mentioned once, as are the concerns held by many about the police chiefs and the Lord Chief Justice being determined to keep police from going anywhere but to the police to blow their whistles. In such a cage corruption can only breed and the lessons of the past can only go unlearned. I see it clearly. People like me are to be treated as witches, either silently drowned or burned, screaming, at the stake. The irony at the day's beginning is that, on my last family outing, we had visited a Castle and seen the dungeons where the Witch Hunter General had once held and tortured many. Much as his methods were acceptable to the then establishment, the methods employed by the PSD are also seen as such.

Following the messages from the union about the potentially unlawful use of interception and phone-hacking - my second irony of the morning having heard the Chief Justice's name again - I can't help but draw a further comparison to the good old W.H.G. His methods were torture, one sided judgement and he often relied on the use of spies and informants to identify his next targets. The PSD use isolation, refusal to communicate or bend, subjective judgement and, it seems, illegal surveillance.

These are harsh and confusing thoughts for the hour but a blog by a retired copper, on the topic of surveillance, is running through my mind.

He made FOI requests to police forces and they refused to provide the information, effectively admitting they use the techniques. This is problematic, not least because the matter for which it may be used must be serious - a crime; a danger to national security. The information runs and runs, and will come back to me later when I am ready to contextualise it all fully, at the leisurely, formative pace of my thoughts. When things have been processed.

Briefly, the voicemail message also flashes through my head. The union Chair for the GLP, tells me they will fund my solicitor after all. On remembering, I breath a second - and less explosive - sigh of relief.

By the time I am at Liverpool Street, outside with a cigarette in one hand and a latte in the other - not so much as glance at Sir Robert, though I am well aware of his presence - I have received some other interesting messages. The first few from friends, worried the PSD may start arresting people willy-nilly following the leaked allegation arrest. The second message is from one of the union's secretaries, from the East of England. He started with a general "what's the state of play?" and "are they still focused on the information?" Then, to my surprise, he said something which actually resulted in raised eyebrows. "I feel partly responsible because union politics mean people like you had to go out on a limb. We're part of the system that justifies them. Doesn't mean what you say means less than if our head honcho had said it. The regs are a gag - end of. Political own goal for force though, clearly been told to silence the barking dogs."

I stare at this and reread it a few times as the pretty girl with the brown hair and blue eyes smiles, pitches her cigarette and heads inside, quickly replaced by two dark skinned chefs and the usual Polish ladies braving the cold in short sleeved blouses. I enjoy one more cigarette and watch the world go by then head into the Central Line - no rush, no crush, and a seat all the way from St Paul's, the second stop. I wonder whether it is Monday or the week before Christmas which has led to this lack of the usual human traffic.

The District is quiet too and then I'm there, inside the tower. Today though, there is a difference, despite the grey cloud bursting with the eerie, orange light of the winter sun, the threat of rain in the air like static. Even as penny-sized raindrops sporadically stop and start in rapid descent I don't feel oppressed by my approach. My heart doesn't change pace and my limbs do not feel the slightest bit leaden. My vision is clear, no frantic dump and crash of adrenaline. My mind, the resilient human brain, aided by the cathartic act of writing, of restructuring and ventilating my thoughts - releasing them from tortuous purgatory - has adapted, or is adapting, to the situation. This is, in action, a precise demonstration of how mankind has become the most dominant and successful creature on the planet. And this is underlined by the frequent occurrences of minds, far from being the rule but which are the example, which fracture with disastrous consequences. That lack of commonality is what punctuates events, such as the latest school shooting in the US. The truly broken human mind is rare, the one undergoing adaptation the most common.

The idea drifts, is lost and then I am in the tower, changing into uniform, no ghostly appearance. Just me.

The first task is an update of map images and statistics, with the DI hanging over my shoulder, wanting to learn how to do it 'in case I am ever not here'. Across the city, in the sun, I catch sight of the London Eye and it appears different, inanimate. Just a wheel and not one upon which I will be broken.

"PSD haven't replied to me yet," he says.

"They've ignored my lawyer three times," I reply. "And libelled me in the national press."

He looks confused. "How's that then?"

I glance at him. "By saying I hadn't raised the issues internally, but you know I did: I raised them with you."

Smirking he turns away.

This is followed by a return phone call to the union Chair, in which he confirms the position on covering legal costs. He actually mentions the wider issues impacting upon all officers - freedom to speak out - is a key concern. I thank him and note down the names of the men at the central office who await receipt of my funding application then leave a voicemail for my local rep, requesting that he sends the form as quickly as possible.

With that, my solicitor's assistant sends me an email. A most curious forward which has been sent regarding me via the firm. I find myself with raised eyebrows for the second time as the officer writing explains his experience, pre-retirement, of mudslinging and bitch fighting - finishing with a flourish by branding the GLP as a vindictive organisation. This is becoming apparently true in my own experience and he offers whatever help he can. Eventually, when I can, I will reply to all of the emails like this which have come through and not only that. I plan to travel the country, interviewing these officers, documenting for the first time this broader view of the service we are all sworn into, or have been. I look forward to that day.

A glance at the message board is very telling indeed, of the tide of anger, disbelief and demoralisation. Many ask about the officer arrested over the leaks, asking the management to show support; questioning proportionality of the arrest on a weekend night; highlighting Code G of the Police and Criminal Evidence Act (which lays down in law the concepts of necessity and proportionality). The officer, I see, has the full backing of the Union, quite contrary to my case in which they have told me and only a handful of others they support me. But then, I had their own politics confirmed to me only hours before.

In another post, 'kettle-rage' continues, as electrical testing prohibits the making of tea in CID offices. Then follows a rumour PSD is to double in size. Finally, there is a real gem, a quote from a Roman Centurion dated 210 BC: "We trained hard but it seemed that every time we were beginning to form up into teams we would be reorganised. I was to learn later in life that we tend to meet any new situation by reorganising; and a wonderful method it can be for creating the illusion of progress while producing confusion, inefficiency and demoralisation." This is as true now as it was over two thousand years ago and, once again, I am struck by the similarities I see between the present and the corrupt end which met Ancient Rome. I wonder though, can't help but do so, if - providing the Mayan calendar proves wrong on the 21st of December - there is still a chance. If, maybe, those old tales of triumph over adversity, of the slave or otherwise underdog making a real difference in the world they are hemmed in by, can still be repeated. If there is still room for the making of new stories or if such things are confined to the past. The centurion suggests not.

With that ancient parity clear in my mind, I find my thoughts heading back over recent history once more, starting with a second look - eyebrows again raised - at the email forwarded from my solicitor. I'd almost overlooked a case highlighted in the opening paragraphs. It mentions a jailed chief officer and reiterates a piece of information I knew about, but which had lost significance in the inevitable tumult of my mental adaptation. When he was a Superintendent, a chief officer no less, he went public in a way which was highly critical of the GLP and was considered very damaging at the time. The result, as highlighted in the email, was that he was promoted. I ponder this for a few moments, then turn my attention to the other piece of recent history which has just made a very public show of itself: the latest of the historic corruption inquiries. The crux of this being the ordered alteration of the statements of operational officers which were critical of either the leadership at the scene – or, more generally, of the chaotic management from superior ranks. All of this was vetted by the legal department with a view to deflecting public blame and anger away from the force and its leadership. This is symptomatic of the broader issues in the police service, of it being a closed door club where blame can only ever be directed at the front line. I think of my case, of the arrested officer, of the message board. I think of one word, which flashes like a bright light, a warning alarm, glowing in the dark and hovering, practically screaming in the air: control.

Control. Control. Control.

The Superintendent, brackets Detective close brackets, sits down next to me, attacking his broken, 'job' mobile with a pair of scissors, desperate to fix the rapidly detaching key pad. I tell him to order a new one but he refuses, continues, and then eventually concedes. Seeing as he is there I ask him if PSD have been in touch with him. He's non committal.

"I spoke to them last week, they're still in a research phase but will be interviewing you in the new year."

"My solicitor has been trying to contact them to no avail."

"Have they, by any chance, replied that they are under no obligation to speak to them or engage at all?"

"No actually," I say and the conversation is over.

In those few words he has said everything there is to say. Not only will they - and are they - fishing for whatever they can find to use against me, but they are also displaying no intent of reviewing the unlawful restriction placed upon me - exercising their absolute discretion to not respond at all. In short, I find myself in a unique situation where I am trapped by a group of people willing to go to any lengths to pin something on me, to make it stick, and, also, I must face this without even common courtesy being extended to my legal defence. As far as the law says I deserve none and, as far as PSD are concerned, they will blindly plough ahead, onwards ever onwards, without thoughts or considerations of anything but control, control, control.

At the moment they have me cornered, while they do what they do, which - if my sources are correct - is mudslinging. Pursuing people vindictively and with malice.

19th December:

After the Detective Superintendent delivered his update, the splendid and resplendent bomb - an exploding bear trap which whistled down from the heavens and exploded at my desk while he absently pulled his phone to pieces - I felt an earthquake. Adrenaline, provided courtesy of the shock, ripped through my limbs leaving my body shaking, my mind an explosion of electrical impulses and my voice box a useless formation of gristle, bone and flesh. Beneath me the floor opened and I felt myself fall, the whole seventeen floors and beyond.

It took me twenty minutes to gain - or regain - enough physical control to put on my fleece and leave the office to smoke. Staggered, stuttering steps. Head down, shoulders loosely hunched. The trap ran through my mind, I played it out, physically clawing at it with the mental projection of myself. I reached for my phone and dialled the number for the Commission for Police Complaints. There is no one else. *There is no one else.*

The woman listens and sounds distressed as she replies, at the end of my long explanation. "I'm really sorry but as you are a serving police officer there is nothing we can do. You need to refer to your own standards people or hope that your solicitor can give you some good advice. I'm really sorry."

I hung up knowing she genuinely was sorry but even so, it did not alleviate the full scale of the trap. Only the police can police the police: as they see fit, by their own rules and in their own court. There is no way out, no other option. In that moment I resigned myself to the expected fate, finished my day and went home, broken.

That night I was unable to write but, in the dark, I prayed. Then I prayed again. Then I slept, much more deeply than I expected. Come morning the sense of being trapped had departed, left no trace and I knew exactly what I had to do.

Yesterday I sat and researched and wrote, wrote and researched, possessed beyond my own expectations and barely distracted by the solicitor providing me the reply from the DI at PSD. The day finished and at home

I wrote more, emailed it back to work again and today carried on.

Taking in the day's news: a police officer sacked for blogging after winning a tribunal as a whistle blower; the Inspectorate of Policing spying on social media and referring issues to forces; the news from the Office of Prosecutions, that common sense would be applied to social media prosecutions. I write and write. Then, there is no more and I hit send. The solicitor, the Union and the head of PSD all get the email simultaneously.

20th December:

The embedded nature of the trap which has protected policing for so long, is sometimes underlined or punctuated by what is reported in the press - like the current corruption inquiry in relation to the allegations against the cabinet minister. It is almost always underpinned by the questionable (yet mostly unquestioned) actions of the senior ranks.

The issue with the minister was incredibly easy to resolve from the outset: they should have been reported for summons and then the evidence would have been put before the

CPS and, possibly, the courts. They in turn would have followed the course of justice. What actually happened is the Prime Minister and Glorious Leader of the GLP appear to have made the joint decision not to allow this to happen. Did they, then, usurp the judiciary? Yes - in doing so breaking one of Robert Peel's cardinal rules. Is this, therefore, the perversion of the course of justice? The thought struck me, looking at the mess surrounding the situation, that yes, a great deal of perversion resulted from the decision. Just look at what followed: perversion from all sides.

The concept is pursued and concluded in the few moments it takes me to order and pay for a latte from the Costa at Liverpool Street station before I head to the solicitor's office to pick up a parcel, left anonymously for me. A lovely Christmas card and two small presents for the children. The wonderful contradiction in this whole situation being the service I love - and was fighting to save - has attacked me for it, whereas the public support (including from many who never before trusted a police officer) is focused on trying to make sure the service recognises it needs challenging people and should fight to keep them.

At the tower I arrive in the office and briefly replay the conversation of the previous afternoon, with the most senior officer in my department.

"Of course, I wrote a book. A practical guide to policing. University Press. They keep asking me about a business interest and submitting the manuscript, but I can't see why I should. I'm sure your stuff will get sorted out."

The words run back through my head while I log on, to see if there has been a response to my email. As I wait, fingers tapping the desk, for the IT to catch up, the Detective Sergeant who bought the trademark stands up to loudly speak, to another M derived officer across the office.

"You're taking over the website because Jack can't be trusted." I look over the top of my screen and he makes eye contact, puts his hand to his mouth and says "Oops."

"Oh, so I can't be trusted then?" I say, noting his lack of reply.

Livid, I email the DCI straight away, highlighting that even the head of PSD had already stated dishonesty was not an issue in my case. Then, rather than let rip on the idiot, I go downstairs and smoke until the rage passes, leaving behind only the emasculating embarrassment.

Back in the office I have a reply, from an Acting Detective Sergeant who is the aforementioned PSD head's staff officer. He is away, so nothing will be done until he gets back. This is a disappointing response. I forward the email to his boss, the deputy chief, asking for it to be actioned. They should, of course, have had a grasp of the issues. Clearly I am wrong, as the staff officer rings me very swiftly to say the deputy has just said they can't reply and I need to wait for the other one's return. I ask for this in writing and in reply I get a further email from another staff officer, a DCI, confirming I will have to wait and mentioning 'personal frustration' on my part. To use the quote in their own, confidentially circulated, report on me: I'm not sure that they 'grasp the seriousness'.

During these hours of back and forth I have started to cough and get hot, meanwhile seeing numerous people dismissed early from the office. At half-four I leave and beyond that there is only a blur as the Influenza grips me with a fever of thirty-nine degrees, uncontrollable shivers, and stabbing aches and pains around my kidneys. I hate being ill, rarely am, and blame the run down of my strong immune system on battle fatigue - the term used by a friend striking me as more apt than he could ever know.

2nd of January:

Walking up to the building retains its almost absolute power of dread and my mind is in a spin, trying to come to terms with a way I can carry on my life as it was before. How to just be able to speak to people, with the same passion. Can I do that without talking about policing? That's what causes the tumult. I visualise a pie chart of me and colour fifty percent of it black; I visualise a black hole, with half of me sucked into it. I visualise my very being as a flat line on a heart monitor. The elephant in the room is so big, years of my life, that there is barely room for anything else.

I drudge up to the doors of the tower in a confused funk. Who the hell am I with fifty percent of me off limits? How can I be myself? Upstairs I log on to the computer and find my inbox devoid of any new mail. No reply. Nothing. Today is the fourteenth since I raised the issues. Today is the fourteenth day of silence in response. Sadly, I decide this just isn't for me anymore and, although I raise an email to my solicitor, expressing all of this and more, I feel the fog descend. I had hoped writing the email would have some sort of positive impact. Rather, I find myself plummeting still, overwhelemed by a feeling of being forced into an impossible situation. A maze where all the ways are shut. Carpe annum seems an unachievable feat.

The good old DI never fails not to disappoint. He wheels his chair towards me and hovers at my shoulder, giving me a list of points he needs covered at a meeting the following day as I book two days of short notice, unpaid leave.

"Can you make sure you send the stuff we need for the meeting?"

I laugh as I comply, forwarding him his own email, with the addition of the requests he made himself, not thirty minutes before. That, right there, is the future of police leadership. At least it raises a smile in the murk I am fighting through, that is until he adds his next nugget.

"I've just had the head of PSD on the phone," the very same one who has now ignored me for two weeks solid. "He's looking at the condition about you speaking to the Home Office but can't see why he should vary it."

I can only imagine the meeting of minds, between current and future leaders, which has just taken place. In fact, so moved am I by the cosmic energy I go downstairs for a cigarette - exhaling each exasperated drag with some vigour. Another Inspector is there, puffing on his electronic cigarette with no less effort.

"This is bullshit," I say and he bends double laughing. "I've never seen anything quite like the GLP's finest, a collection of self-serving, self-interested buffoons."

"Ah, but we call it ambitious!" he replies, still laughing. I join him, taking out my fury on the cigarette.

More than ever I am convinced this will end with me suffering from PTSD and, as if I needed to be further convinced, I then receive a phone call from the Resourcing Office - that pinnacle of effective working at my old unit: the place I haven't worked at for over nine months.

"We'll take a day of annual leave from you for New Year's Eve, you didn't come in and you are still shown as a local resource." I think of the Titanic and lost souls.

"Couldn't have if I'd wanted to, I have a load of restrictions on me at the moment." "What for?" they ask.

"You'd best Google my name and GLP."

I thought I would have ceased to be amazed by now, nonetheless I find myself struck by a whole new rush of awe. Briefly I wonder how this organisation has survived so long, then arrive at the only explanation: a combination of lucky necessity and self-preservation.

As a final hoot, I open the homepage and take a look at the 'GLP Press Coverage' section. Apparently it is important for transparency and public confidence they show they are 'here for London' and reply to questions. I stifle a laugh, a real bray.

The carousel continues to spin and spin, sickeningly so. My next email is from the staff officer again. This time the rocking horse wants to tell me a story which is by now very familiar: a response is being given consideration. So surprised am I that no reaction, of any kind, is elicited whatsoever.

Later, on my personal email, I receive some news I welcome. My solicitor is back from holiday, is reading through emails, and wants to meet in the office on Friday. I resolve myself to an evening of printing and hole punching but feel much better, even though I know the subject of funding will come up and I am not the proud possessor of more than a voluntarily repossessed house. I squirm at the thought, which recurs, but manage to make it through the afternoon and away.

Waiting for the tube I have the misfortune to read a blathering, blithering blog, of a Superintendent, on the topic of social media. The hopelessness boils over.

Just then, just right then, my QC calls. Can I condense what evidence I would give to a Parliamentary Select Committee into a couple of paragraphs? And, would I be willing to give evidence?

Oh God Yes.

7th of January:

This morning I can feel it, all of it, the pressure of it all bearing on me. No just from above but from all angles.

My best friend once told me about the last recording from a sinking submarine; the sound of the hull imploding – screams; rivets exploding like bullets. He was nonchalant, my friend, as he explained this, primarily because it had been his life. For me that growing, crushing pressure may not be a physical threat but it is no less dangerous, because it is happening to my mind. What is being done to me is inhumane and yet...and yet, I have boarded the early train anyway.

All the way, since waking up at five, I have fought the urge inside me - the urge to stay at home, climb into my shell and stay there. Increasingly I want people to go away. This tells me things are reaching crisis point. The helplessness of being in a hopeless situation and still not feeling entirely hopeless, reverberates through the hull of my being. I want to retreat into that deep, lonely well. I once drilled for it, forced it to exist, but now I know it is there and calling out to me: begging me to come down into the dark comfort so I can be safe while I replenish the strength which drives me. Part of me does worry if I do go to that inside place my need will be so great I may stay there. Just stay. Another part of me feels this time I am being pushed, forced into the abyss, exactly by the design of others. For this reason I resist, unwilling to be water-boarded in my own soul. Which is quite precisely how this feels.

Even Friday's meeting with the solicitor had failed to resolve the internal turmoil, which dredged more of its own silt over the course of the weekend. In this, the union are causing as much pressure as others. At the end of the meeting, I left with my rucksack significantly lighter and with a couple of fresh thoughts in mind. If I give evidence to the Committee, of police corruption, I will be breaching my restrictions. I made clear it is imperative to give the evidence, but the brief says nothing - which leaves the ball firmly in my court. Rightly, as they are not blessed with a magic wand, the decision must be mine. I have ignored it over the weekend. I must now think again and, on the train with the darkness as an envelope on the world outside, I arrive at a decision.

My decision is to ask for permission to attend and give evidence. You see, that way, the GLP will finally have to take some responsibility: whether it be to have the balls to do the right thing, or the balls to hide corruption from the public.

At Liverpool Street I don't even look at Sir Robert, I feel too embarrassed for him - for what his creation has become. I smoke two cigarettes and text the legals, seeking their approval to ask permission - an inherently odd request to have to make as an adult. I highlight this lays the decision on the GLP and doesn't breach my conditions. The text makes me think of speaking to the union Chair over the weekend - he asked how I was. I told him I had been humiliated and was within minutes of resigning.

The exchange was prompted because I used social media to say rest in peace to two former colleagues, taken on to the next life by cancer. For that I don't care about the restrictions. As I said to a friend: "the day I don't pay my respects openly is the day the world can kiss my ass." The union man didn't reply to the text about humiliation but then, how do you deal with that kind of raw truth? Human emotion makes most blokes go a rubbery one.

As I'm pondering this, a book being read on the tube, catches my eye - the title "He Kills Coppers." Upside down I read that there are two types of corrupt persons: meat-eaters and grass-eaters. The former actively seeks out opportunity for personal gain, the latter simply accepts whatever comes their way. The author is called Jake, I can't see the surname as it's obscured by fingers. Silently I applaud him for hitting the nail on the head. In my opinion there are equally two types of non-corrupt persons: the grass-eaters and the meat-eaters. The former will simply graze on whatever is obvious in front of them, slowly chewing it over. The latter hunt out corruption with ravenous delight and, even if the prey is bigger than they are, they will try and bring it to the ground anyway. Writing this I feel a flush, the first positively framed adrenaline rush for five weeks or more. A stark contrast to the overwhelming urge to throw up on the painful tower approach.

Unexpected and expected events fill my day.

It begins with a text message from the DI just after nine, talking of a meeting I knew nothing about, which was to start at half past. Unexpected was his addition that PSD had lifted the restriction on speaking to the two men from the Home Office, so I could actually do my job. I feel no elation and remain skeptical even when reading the Detective Superintendent's somewhat vague explanation as to why the head of PSD had agreed to vary the condition.

Still a cynic, but now prepared to plumb the depths of ineptitude, I take a free dive and call the PSD Detective Inspector who is investigating me. She sighs grumpily as she hears my name - *sorry, but you applied for the job* - and request confirmation of the amendment. She hasn't been 'sighted of any.' I find her reply almost makes me laugh and struggle to hold it in.

I quickly email the solicitor, pointing out that I am now on a project and allowed to speak to the two people I was forcibly humiliated in front of only weeks ago. Control, plus Alt, plus Delete locks my screen and away I go to the upper floor conference rooms, where I speak privately to the shorter Home Office man. He is all ears, and I apologise in advance for any distracted moments of staring out of the window, to which I am now prone. I don't mention the likely clangs of my hull being crushed, or bangs as the rivets pop like machine gun fire.

The meeting drags, a regular festival of ego and buzzword bingo which I find depressing, although I do manage to speak up during this. Once to make sure we have to include and deal with perversion of burglary figures (and all that brings) and then to make sure we don't just fudge our working hours as the DCI suggests - the law requires they are dealt with in a certain way, after all. The idea he put forward was vague, at best: for us to possibly, maybe, have odd hours off.

At lunch I tell the DI that I urgently need to request permission to give evidence at the Committee but we fall at the first hurdle as, even unabbreviated, he doesn't know what a Select Committee is. Though I need not his prompt, he tells me to email the head of PSD direct. I'm feeling brave so I even put a deadline for reply, of half past four.

A couple of hours later my reply arrives, from the staff officer: their boss would like some more detail. I tell him, via them, I want to discuss ethical crime recording and crime pattern analysis, evidence based change management and promotion processes, and the current provisions for whistleblowing by serving officers. Strangely, my deadline passes without response.

Just after half-three I see the variation of my restrictions for the first time. I wonder how the project will be, when a primary function is 'stakeholder engagement' - we are actually talking about this all day tomorrow.

I finish the day, pausing at the station only to text the QC who replies straight away, to make clear the deadline for submissions is tomorrow. I take this to mean tomorrow is the last day of evidence being accepted.

I feel sick heading home and get there to the sounds of my little girl crying. I go upstairs to settle her and in my arms she begins to relax then, *Ding!* My phone goes off with a text. She wakes up fully, pokes me in the eye, pinches my nose, then does a poo.

"Caca," she proudly announces. It looks as if she has been eating Play-Doh again. As I change her nappy, she looks out of the cot and, laughing, shouts the word "Do-How!"

"Yes!" I tell her. "It is your Doll's House." With that there is a shuffling behind me, as the boy stacks up the foam number-tiles, climbs on top of the pile, and switches on the light.

"Hello Daddy!"

For the next half hour the three of us hide in a tent - the boy's duvet - until they fall asleep.

I successfully lie in bed awake until two in the morning, then have a nightmare about hoovering and feel awful when the alarm goes off at five. I interpret the dream as a craving for more mundane types of stress, more boring pressures. Given the last few years, the fact this comes as a surprise is startling in itself.

8th of January:

It is now the reverse journey, homeward bound. First on the grubby, red-liveried train of the Central Line.

This morning I got to work at twenty-to-nine and logged on to find an email from the head of PSD himself, sent at half-seven the previous evening. Why he chose not to use the personal contact details I provided will forever remain a mystery. He almost thanked me in the message, for asking permission to give evidence to Parliament, then declined to grant it on the basis it doesn't form part of my 'normal duties'. I'm unaware of anyone who's day job is to do anything of the sort. But telling the truth is central to being a police officer, you might think. He also bravely - yet foolishly I felt - lied by proxy. He stated my line manager, the DI, was unaware. It's funny because I clearly remember him not knowing what the Committee was. I forwarded this to the solicitor immediately and also made arrangements for one of the witnesses of the conversation to get in touch and make a statement. I knew lies were inevitable, just not so openly. Or so soon.

Feeling shocked but also bolstered by their predictability, I went upstairs for the second, very interesting, day of the project. It smashed by fast. First I was put in charge of base-lining, gathering the evidence of current performance. I accounted for finance, resource management and the perversion of crime levels and detection rates. I was moaned at repeatedly with each turn, so made my point bluntly: "The figures are perverse bullshit, you all know it. So, we either deal with it once and for all or everything we do, in the end, will perpetuate perverse bullshit."

They settled on the idea the manipulation and perversion which goes on should be seen as harmless 'loop-hooling' - otherwise it implies wrongdoing. *Implies?*

I persisted so much they offered to put me outside on the window cleaning rig, where I could be seen and not heard.

At the end - and when we were alone - the short civil servant told me he understood that picking the thread of bent figures could unravel the whole service and all who have risen through the ranks on meeting targets. We both knew it wouldn't happen, of course. Not unless someone pulled the fraying fabric. But in that lies but half of the issue: the choice itself. The decision of police officers to bend the figures, to meet the targets, to get promoted. Choice to let it carry on. My own choice: to do my best to tell the truth. With that comes indeterminable pain. In the main, the hurt comes from knowing that telling it has not only the potential to damage you but hurt your family too.

The prospect of becoming unemployed by virtue of the closed arrangements within the police, is terrifying. Nothing less than terrifying.

Yet I have made my bed and now must lie in it.

9th of January:

When I wake up my head is still spinning.

Through the tiredness a dull throb of a headache sits on my forehead, just above my nose. My eyes ache, but I am awake and thinking with no respite. More of yesterday comes back to me. A whirlwind of thoughts, even as I make coffee in my pyjamas...

Aside from the perverse bullshit of statistics, manipulated for personal gain - the thread which could unravel the whole police service - we had discussed stakeholders, identifying all who would have interest in - and influence over - the project. The word stakeholders was mentioned hundreds of times: we must engage with them, talk to them, observe them, mentor them, guide and drive them. Before we finish I mentioned the elephant.

"Erm...because of the poorly worded and absolute restrictions I have, I can't have contact with stakeholders." After staring, gormless, for a second he without basic knowledge of parliamentary committees, the Detective

Inspector, replied.

"We'll, when we do the consultation phase, you can just do the back office stuff." I stare at him. A buffoon in a suit.

"But it says 'no contact', so I can't be involved in the actual project phase, day in the life studies, on site assessments...."

He stares blankly, not comprehending and then leaves, without further comment.

Thoughts of the Committee whirl, muddled, again.

The Detective Constable from the PSD has replied - she would like me to pick a date for the interview quickly and, when she has booked a room, she'll 'send me something'. I ask in reply if my solicitor can be present but expect no response as the DC is off for the day.

I head up to the project room and spend the morning identifying ways to engage with stakeholders I can't engage with. I talk about social media, mainstream media and the basic principles of successful micro-blogging. They make crass jokes and are dismissive. A room full of idiots, out of their depths and out for their own interests.

Briefly, I read the London Mayor's draft plan

for policing, seeing the built in figure-fiddles straight away. I read a brilliant briefing about the astounding crime reductions this year. All of this settles my resolve, the truth about figures - confirmed yet again by a new DCI - must come out. For the first time in weeks I think clearly and loudly that the public deserve much more than spin and grass-eating.

I am tired, yes; resigned to the fact the job I love wants me silent, maybe out to boot, but...but: I am alive in every ounce of my being. I take the trains and settle into The Histories, lost in the world of Herodotus as I travel.

10th of January:

It is, I think, the constant yo-yo of emotions which is doing the most damage.

As in the beginning, adrenaline slams across my poor, weight-dropping body in the harshest waves. When this is done, however this ends, I will need more sleep than I have ever needed in my life. To have this happening to you, with no respite, to feel what it is doing to you...

This calmly exits from my mind to the page as I sit in the relaxed Starbucks on Fleet Street, ten seconds from the door to the legal offices where I am waiting for our meeting. I have already concluded we will decide to let the Greater London Police follow whatever course they choose. The punishment of intimately understanding an organisation and having the ability to interpret law and procedure is that you become prescient of what happens next.

I was called that - *prescient* - last night, after a friend read the full article on the GLP closing police stations, moving to supermarkets, and juggling staff into neighbourhood policing teams. I think over everything I have said and written about this and dismiss prescience in favour of the predictions being based upon knowledge, understanding, and sound logic. Albeit true that logic is harder to maintain while on this roller-coaster.

A giant poster of freshly picked coffee beans idly distracts me for about ten seconds, before I realise I am staring vacantly and correct myself. I try to focus on what I would say exactly, if set before MPs. But the thought is blocked. Dependent on the hope others will deliver me into such salvation.

My eyes are once again stinging from the pain of constant focus and from reading

Herodotus - the names and places a constant, alien interruption, often causing a furrowed brow as I strain for concentration in distraction. In losing myself in the history of our world. I realise, so far, I recognise most of the tales but, above all else, I recognise that human nature has fundamentally changed very little. Greed, corruption, deviance, dealing, riches, self-interest, coup. Love, passion, and heroic acts. We may have evolved in terms of technology, but we are no different. No change since around five hundred years before the God I know as Christ came about. Human nature, designed or evolved as it was to preserve itself first and foremost, has remained the driving factor. And remains the reason it is elephants - and not us - dying in the dry desert at the foot of Kilimanjaro. At times the weight of generations of so called humanity bears down on all of us like the axe does on a block.

My day is as productive as can be: I suffer the afternoon listening to clowns justify why they may fail in carrying out a review of a process. Worse still, hearing that the northern police force - from whence the amazing rock of our Glorious Leader came -

was subject to a poor performance notice by the Inspectorate just before he was appointed in London as the great champion of policing. I am worried. For the others it appears to be par for the course.

I also have a reply, four weeks later, from PSD - effectively saying they are doing nothing. Nothing at all about the issues I've challenged them about.

Being in the hands of others is no place to be. Not for one minute, one month or, over six weeks. This is because everything our race has taught me about itself and everything documented about it over thousands of years is absolutely undeniable. Only I can give a true account of myself, because others will do as they please.

11th of January:

Last night, walking up the dimly lit street which marks the last metres of the road home, I began to cry in frustration. I couldn't help it and nor could I stop the words which spilled from my mouth as I did it. "All I did was tell the truth."

About an hour later, while my wife was in the kitchen clattering around with something, I cried again. Involuntarily. I do not like to cry and rarely engage in the activity.

Subsequently, when I woke up in the morning, not only was I feeling humiliated but a cold, quiet anger - the most dangerous form of it there is - began to run through me. For years now I have been living this nightmare, going well beyond the boundaries in which many contain themselves; beyond the grazing plains where the grass-eaters dwell. There has been and will be no let up for me and, on every occasion where I feel or have felt some breakthrough was either close or actually being made, I have received one form of sucker punch or another. On every occasion I have come to terms with it and been able to drag myself up, onto my feet, and forwards once more. As things stand now I am being pushed to an edge from which I don't know the distance of the fall, or if I will be able to get back up.

In the catharsis of writing this, expelling it from my mind, I feel that cold anger begin to grow. I cannot stop it. Once there it will do as it needs to protect me - part of the human survival mechanism built into each and every one of us.

Today, after a brief assembly of the project team, my focus has been upon the forthcoming interview. It is not so far away and at least I have somewhere to aim. A fixed date before a further wait.

Rather than lunch I decide to sit at my desk and pick out what I need, for now. I check the DC's email once more: she hasn't disclosed what I am alleged to have done and, by her own admission, is not entirely ready for the interview. Neither of these scenarios are compatible with even the PSD's own guidance. The former - lack of disclosed information - is contrary to the requirement to provide me with specific allegations, times and dates of the alleged conduct. She hasn't specified anything. Secondary is the issue of the reason for the interview - again their own guidance saying it must be proportionate and necessary, and so forth. My question would therefore be, *if you are still preparing, do you actually know what I am supposed to have done?* Ergo, is it necessary? Since I first was told of the intent to 'fact-find' - four weeks before formal investigation began - this entire mess has smacked of fishing trip. It is completely by virtue of these thoughts of procedures I arrive at a key element of my initial interview plan: policy.

Earlier in the year I had declined, by virtue of the farce of it, to take part in the redesign of the entire system of Standard Operating Procedures commissioned by the boss himself. In essence, it had become apparent policy and procedure within the GLP was 'unwieldy, verbose and unusable'. I double check my recollection of this with another officer in the open plan who is working on the continuance of this project. To my utter delight he uses words like *conflicting* and *confusing*, and gives examples - including one of thirty-two fatal failures in the performance procedures arising from poor interpretation. So poor, in fact, the policy had drifted away from the actual law it was based upon. Timely as ever, this reminds me of the case of a smaller force, who had been overruled in a decision on a dismissal because they relied on Home Office policy guidance, rather than the regulations. Which is the law itself. The very reason for the existence of policy.

No other news comes. Not necessarily good news but, to be frank, I craved the rest having been tired and strung out enough to repeatedly fall asleep over the course of the weekend.

Aside from policy, I am hung up on the thought of this morning on the Central Line as the doors opened at Notting Hill Gate: "An institution which lies to the public is no good to the public. An organisation which lies to itself is no good to anybody." This portent, at half-past-eight or thereabouts, served three times during the rest of the day.

At the Committee - where I was not giving evidence, having been declined permission - the chiefs whittled about the importance of ethics in police leadership. I can tell you there are some, but only when or for as long as it suits. I didn't pay too much attention as I was busy with the base-lining of burglary nationally and across the GLP. All ways I look at it, with the sheer amount of manipulation that goes on there is no way I can say any of it is accurate and, even within what is there, it contradicts itself. There are so many versions of the truth it's almost hopeless. Yet I do my best and come up with a reasonable result: things are worse in London than elsewhere but all of it is questionable.

The third and final thing was about the

public order officers who were accused of - and charged with - racially motivated criminal offences. The copper on the nearest desk to my island is fast becoming as effective as the oracle at Delphi once was. With my ongoing readings of The Histories fresh in my mind, absorbed in that world as I am - in calls from the ill-destined king, Xerxes, for earth and water; of corrupt governments and tyrants; of self preserving deals to be done - the oracle speaks and I listen. It transpires these officers, acquitted as innocent by the courts by virtue of CCTV footage, were almost condemned by virtue of the same footage which, proving their innocence, was withheld from the court by PSD. Yes, the same Professional Standards Department of the GLP who 'might' use questionable surveillance, of which the union are well aware.

At court, it seems, the then Commissioner said "I have no doubt these men are guilty." They were subsequently left to pick through several thousand hours of footage themselves to prove their innocence and rectify the deceit perpetuated and hidden by the very people charged with upholding standards inside the police. It seems that an injustice escaped being done by a whisker. How many more cases have their been? Will there be? I ponder this briefly, only briefly, determined not to ruin my otherwise good and normal mood.

Once again, as the day ends, I have arrived at the station early enough to have a seat on the train. The novelty of this, particularly in my current state of emotional yo-yo, is well received and I even remove my coat - a token of my relaxed state as I exhale the filthy air of the last week. I am not the same, sobbing, overwrought man I was last night and, although the cold anger, present only hours ago, has not gone, it is behaving itself. Being productive in its existence, steadying me and making sure the emotions, overwhelming as they may be, are focused on the task in hand.

I have not yielded to silence, I have adapted to it. About my character, with which I must sleep nightly, this has given me great reassurance. I am still me and, world be damned, I will continue to be. Even as trains thunder beside each other. Even as deals are done, as buttocks go numb, people forget, questions are glossed over, and lies are told. Even as battles are lost and people preserve themselves, I will still be me.

15th January:

"Without opportunity, greed is useless."

Words which I am glad I captured before bed as, when I awake again, they are gone - replaced rather by a sense of peace, knowledge I truly can exist without even a thought as to the huge element of my life which has been wrenched from me. It wasn't so long ago I struggled to find a way I could go on, with something which dominates every aspect of my life off the table. And now? This morning I feel the crystal clear instruction I must follow is to de-institutionalise myself.

While some may interpret this as giving up, it isn't. Having plunged myself into the dark underbelly of my organisation, what I must do - once again and in order to survive - is to see the wood for the trees. The plan is clunky around this, I give you, but the pressing need, the screaming exigency as I awake, is to do it. In part, I suppose, it could be to prevent the experience from making me hate what I love and stand for, although I don't think so. What has wrapped its clawed hands around me resembles little of what I represent. Hate is something of which I must be mindful, though. I have no desire to get lost in smites and begats of more wrongdoing.

In the freezing street, walking to the bus, which is invariably late, I say my prayers out loud: the Lord's Prayer, a once lost memory of childhood, and then the Servant's prayer - which popped up - and there is no other way to explain it - on a mountain top. The chill wind blows, comforting around me, losing its teeth.

Thus far today I have succeeded in establishing that a Sergeant and Inspector, with combined experience of over fifty years in the GLP a) do not fully understand the full process of crime investigation and b) that by comparison to officers from other forces they have a significant skills deficit, which has needed to be addressed since the beginning of time. This no longer surprises me but I am stunned to learn I am no longer depressed by this. Fundamentally, my new found inner peace is telling me this is no longer my personal burden to carry. I find the entire experience rather liberating.

Wryly amusing is the launch of the GLP's robbery campaign, in which they continue to refer to the offence of 'snatch' which does not exist. So blatant is the manipulation that will one day be discovered, to the great discomfort of many. Again though, my peace is not disturbed.

I think, in part, that because I have told the truth (privately and publicly too) the burden is no longer on me. I have done everything I possibly can and, while the hands of others caused me such great disturbance in the last few weeks, I realise their hands will be the ones bloodied in the end. Even the Home Secretary's acceptance of the latest reforms, in full, does not disturb me. The deluded voices which finally speak when it is too late are from those who must take this weight. Whatever events now unfold I have done, in this aspect of my life, as much as I can for now. Although, admittedly, I expect this respite to be at best temporary.

Having concluded the morning's session, in which I learned just how little others have learned, and before correcting an error in the data of the risk report relating to the inclusion of airport data disturbing automated formulae - I have been under a bit of distracting pressure and have never claimed to be perfect - the whole department attends a meeting. We are first spoken to by a manager from forensics, who trumpets increases in the work of Scenes of Crime Officers, then proves my earlier point once more by launching into a tirade to the effect that detectives simply do not know how to investigate crime: not staging disclosure nor being able to interpret even basic forensic evidence like the position of fingerprints. Then comes the turn of the Superintendent charged with developing and implementing standardised 'Control Hubs', across the capital. Essentially he has unified working practices, but the model does not have to be taken up, in short creating a spurious, voluntary scheme to be implemented in over thirty different ways, but providing excellent evidence for his own promotion.

Lastly, we have my very own Detective Superintendent talking us through the Neighbourhood Policing Model. It isn't being piloted or tested, but will be implemented across London in May or June. Maybe. It takes staff from response teams and puts them on Safer Neighbourhood Teams, showing the public a commitment to expanding community policing while at the same time giving them a portion of the work from the teams they are being taken from and, it seems, quite a bit of work from the squads which will also be disbanded. I simply see the evolution of the remit culture ad infinitum and some cheap parlour tricks. Officer numbers to be publicly spun.

With the day done, I devour the last pages of book nine of Herodotus, learning in the end that, while hard men may come from hard country, they may fall when greed and anger make them act. Even when faced with the often lazy, or those of questionable moral fibre.

Aside from the eye-watering, headache-inducing, nature of his long winded expeditions into the naming of family trees mid-paragraph, he makes an excellent companion to train and tube travel. His world is fascinating, his observations on humanity startlingly modern. One day I may stand at Delphi, to listen for the echoes of a real oracle, or on the battleground of Platea, to feel underfoot the soil where thousands met and died. To picture the seamless skull of the Persian over seven feet tall, or the Hoplites under attack from the spring-trampling cavalry. One day I may do this, or travel by boat to see the Hellespont or the pillars of Heracles. One day. But not now. I realise that I have my own piece of history, which - when written down - sounds as far-fetched as the stories of dog-headed men and the Gods walking amongst the general public. My history is recent and as yet unknown - though now, in this peace, I feel more confident than ever I can tell it properly, fairly and honestly. I suppose, in many ways, the way which I have devoured Kafka, Kerouac, Carver and Herodotus in the last few weeks has been my own way of regrouping, by way of the tales of others, before telling my own.

16th January:

Standing on the frozen platform, a hot cup of coffee in my left hand warming my palm as the knuckles, facing the chill wind, burn with cold, I gratefully hop on the train and settle in my usual seat - right leg warming slowly against the weak heater.

I open my next read, Dante's Divine Comedy. Immediately, in the description of the lower rings of his conical Hell - the eighth circle containing the deceitful and swindlers in public office, and the ninth containing the treacherous, false to kindred, country and cause - I see familiarity and nod gently in real understanding. Many of those I have encountered are destined to these circles forever more.

Tonight I will be meeting the legals, to discuss my case, to plan for the interview which, I have discovered, I will be attending without even a union rep, as my appointed one has taken a day off. Not that he would be much use in any case, knowing less about the regulations, it appears, than I now do. Briefly this leads me to think on the constitutional change I see necessary to the Union.

At present, the reps are the only ones who have votes - a voice effectively - in deciding who is elected to the central committees, who in turn represent over 100,000 officers. Subsequently they tend to represent their own interests and agendas in their selections - this being no insult, just a fact of human nature which has shown constant throughout history. If given the option and taking into account the democratic centre of the new policing world, that being the new Commissioners, perhaps the committee members should be voted in by all cops.

That sordid affair with the minister was an

utter farce from the outset but, before
getting to the union, it's important to restate
the key problem. Had Glorious Leader and
the Prime Minister, rather than step in
immediately, allowed evidence to be
gathered following the allegation, then this
whole matter would have been put before
the judiciary - as is quite proper - rather
than it being tried in the court of public and
political opinion in the tent of a media
circus. The result: the puerile actions of a
faction of the Union, unelected by officers
and performing of their own accord. Rather
than represent, they tainted all officers and it
is time for constitutional change.

The thought passes.

Bollocks is a good word to describe what was
spoken at this morning's process mapping
session - in which two detectives of rank
failed to explain, in any way, the exact order
in which they have to structure their work.
In fact, what was established is I am the only
person in the room who appears to
understand the simple process to be
followed when investigating crime. I am
concerned by this. Not least because, by
virtue of position achieved through selection
processes (and the now national, work-based

assessment model), these two detectives are alleged to be the cream of the crop. The session thankfully finished at lunch time, leaving me to work on base-lining again and I have found myself in strange territory, heading to the analysts to check some discrepancies.

I walk away learning that, in October, a report was produced showing a crime reduction of 3.6% but, by January, the same report showed a reduction of 5%, clearly showing the disappearance of several hundred burglaries from the crime figures (and this without considering that around 5% of crimes, initially classified as burglary, were being immediately re-jigged). So, we have quick adjustment and also longer term adjustment of crime figures. Once again my suspicions are confirmed but, really, my heart isn't in this.

Not even the email from the solicitor, stating the Union have formally agreed to fund legal representation - albeit only until a ten hour cap is reached - manages to raise a smile.

At least, later, I will be able to find out how many of these hours I have left until I am on my own.

18th January:

I walk into the chambers of my QC and meet him for the first time. A stout man, he is shorter than I expected but, perhaps as you would hope, very QC like. We size each other silently and, I believe this goes for both of us, decide to reserve judgement until the conference. He retires to await the solicitor, having expressed his concern the giant fish tank behind the reception desk needs more fish. I learn via the receptionist four have died in the last week. Even my presently over prophetic mind sees nothing in this, no portent of doom.

The solicitor arrives just as I finish my latte from the Costa on Chancery Lane and I wait five minutes or so, having watched them both go inside with the toddler sized folders I have provided over the last few weeks. The QC returns, then leads me to the basement meeting rooms where I mutter apologies about casual dress and the receptionist brings coffee, which the solicitor pours.

As a trio we agree as long as I avoid the topic of policing - the large percentage of my life I have worked through being able to live without - then I can be normal once more and even use social media too.

With that I am back in the real world. I reflect on this with some irony, writing an online message even as I walk out of the door. The result is a large volume of replies I am no longer accustomed to keeping up with. I resolve to be human and nothing more. I'm not sure people will follow things so closely or with such interest without the policing twist but the initial response is positive and, frankly, we'll have to suck it and see as I have no real choice in the matter for now.

I realise something. Since all this began, this is the first relatively normal thing I have even worried about for more than five minutes. This is a sign the peace felt at the start of the week is still present and not only that, but normality is returning against all odds, contrary to what I believed only weeks ago. Far from out of the woods though I am, I feel more like me and, best of all: I am finding there is much outside of the job that has so consumed me. My soul feels freer than at any point I can really remember. This may come and go, I may falter, but I now feel confident I can be de-institutionalised.

Yesterday, due to an overhead line fault, all

my trains to London were cancelled and then delayed so, rather than infinitely waste hours travelling and waiting, screwing up a ball of working day and throwing in the bin, I took a decision to go home and work from there. Quite a responsible move and, taking into account I only had research to do, it was quicker. Of course, this may have generated some consternation at work. The DI, had what I can only call, a right old strop about it. That was his most productive contribution to the meeting this morning, a gathering with the Home Office for a detailed update on the project. Aside, of course, from the prolific repetition of the word *erm*, for which I may throttle him one day.

"Who did you call to say you weren't going to be in the office?"

"Well, I told you, by text, as you know."

He mutters that he asked me to call someone else.

"And I told you, I didn't have the numbers."

Bizarrely, when it seems due to sleet the whole department is dismissed, the last of them leaving at about half-eleven. I am the last to leave, allegedly the naughtiest of the naughty. I can't help but walk out with a spring in my step and a smile on my face. I understand this game, I understand the players and, above all else, I completely understand myself.

There is a fight coming and just going into it with this knowledge can only mean that I'm now prepared as can be.

21st January:

As an intrepid explorer I set out in the snow, which crunches underfoot, and make my way to the bus stop where I proceed to wait for a significant amount of time, missing two trains in the process, and eventually arrive in London very late.

The tube is grubby, grit-salt water puddling across the entire floor, miserable, sneezing commuters occupying all space. By the time we pass Bond Street I am starting to feel the doom and gloom of the approaching day, the tower making its presence felt, even underground.

I have no idea what the hours ahead will bring, and with one week to go until the interview I am genuinely not in the mood for any of the inevitable cobblers which will occur between now and then. Purposefully, I am keeping my thoughts away and yet, in the pit of my stomach, the trepidation which was absent in the snow has a keen presence - a knotted snake wriggling around in my guts and spitting venomous anxiety. The stations tick by. Lancaster Gate: the urge to turn around now overwhelming. Queensway: no desire to put on the uniform I am no longer proud of. No desire to see those people who live a lie which doesn't have the redeeming features of being good fiction.

In other areas too people are becoming a bit much, too demanding, selfish. Pushy. My need to retreat from humanity is, at present, a noose around my neck. I will fight through this latest wave, of course. But time is what I need. Time, coffee, cigarettes and space. Three out of four, with space impossible, will have to suffice. The tower looms. And, in the end, the tower disappoints.

Yet again the morning is a bust: another project meeting. With only three of us turning up, we meander aimlessly around and I walk away from it with a baseline of corrupted figures to finish and a baseline of more department-specific figures to commence. Taking into account the whole week is meetings I successfully manage to procure three hours tomorrow morning to actually do some work rather than talk about doing it.

I spend the afternoon settling into the final draft of my statement for the coming interview and, aside from it being sent to the solicitor to review, leave the tower none the wiser than I was when I walked in.

22nd January:

Having not slept - at first through simply not being able to shake threads of thoughts which have to be written down, then through a nightmare in which my teeth rotted away in seconds, a further nightmare about two of my friends being kidnapped and stabbed while on duty and, finally, through having to eject the boy from my bed and back into his own - I find I am not at my most coherent. To add insult to injury, the bus is late enough to prevent me buying a cup of coffee to wake me up. However, I sit writing then come to a natural pause, where Hemingway's perfectly described well is getting dry and it is time to rest. To let it replenish.

The first steps of the morning prove to be no disappointment. I am taken up to the auditorium on the top floor by a man who claims to be a friendly Inspector. He needs my help with colour adjustment on two images, nestled within a detailed presentation on how the department will function. Smiling he unveils it. My framework and escalation scale, developed back in June last year and under my own steam, which will form the basis of the entire structure and function of our department. Key to this are my risk reports which feed the entire process. The flip side of seeing this presentation is that I am not acknowledged anywhere: others will take the credit and doubtlessly gain their promotions. Rather than become frustrated, I decide having had this level of influence is good enough.

I return to the open plan, briefly looking out over snow capped London. The office is in chaos as another department moves onto the floor. I have no idea who they are or what function they perform. Someone mumbles the DI is looking for me and I am directed to the office where his brother sits. Both of them are there, Tweedles Dum and Dee, huddled next to each other. I stand in the doorway and without introduction the

DI snaps: "Maps."

"Maps?" I reply, somewhat confused.

"Yes maps, every Monday. Traceable liquids." I'd forgotten due to the baselining of the project, which I had the first real opportunity to get on with yesterday afternoon.

"Oh balls," I say. "I'll do it now."

"We need to talk about your sickness. Four times in twelve months." Again he is snappy.

I sigh and respond with a simple but short, "Now?"

He says later and I plod back to my desk, sit and write the conversation down in my A4 notepad, then open my sickness record on the HR system. From early April two years ago to last April I was not sick once. I had three days off, with a vomiting bug in May last year, one day off in August with what appeared to be the flu - I was actually sent home from duties by an Inspector rather than taking the day off. In early September I had two days off on the advice of my GP, due to an unusual attack of stress related arrhythmia - which actually came about when I realised the system was strongly weighted towards silence and self-preservation. I may not take much advice but I don't argue with doctors, not being a medical professional myself - ask me one on Crack Houses. Lastly, there was my bout of the flu over Christmas, which resulted in the loss of one working day, two rest days, one day of annual leave, and a bank holiday; namely Christmas Day. Of course, who am I to point out the last was brought about directly by the GLP putting me in a dark and stressful place which destroyed my immune system and my ability to even think straight?

In many ways I am glad to have been writing this for a few weeks. I have the history of this period down on paper, written as it happened. I look forward to the conversation with the DI, to see what else can be done to deal with such a problematic individual as myself. As I sit at my desk he comes and hovers, blatantly reading the notes I have made, not even bothering to disguise it. His presence makes me want to scream. There's a brief pause, where nothing at all occurs and then I receive an email from the Surveillance Commission. There is nothing they can do for me, it seems, however they direct me to another agency in the chain. Another Commission which can do nothing. It is no wonder so much corruption takes place: there are simply no channels which can be simply followed to expose or deal with it. So far, I have found the police, the Union, the Police Authority, the Mayor's Office, the Home Secretary, the Serious Fraud Office, the Complaints system and the Surveillance Commission are not the appropriate authorities to deal with any of this mess. This maze of dead ends no longer damages me as it possibly should.

The DI beckons me into the office towards the end of lunch, which I haven't taken again. It appears dealing with someone who writes things down and knows what they are talking about does have an effect: he recaps my sickness, states he understands the stress impact of misconduct investigations and, after a rather uncomfortable *what can I do to help?*, resolves he has no further issues. I conclude I dislike him most of all because, at present, he is the only visible point of contact I have with the PSD, who I now refer to as the Voice of the Mysterons. That's part of it. Part. The other piece is simply I don't like him on gut instinct. Regardless, I don't hold any of it against him personally.

29th January:

It begins at about ten-past-one, in a boiling hot room on the twenty-second floor, in the entrance way to the gents lockers rooms. If I was a psychologically masterminding this, then I would use this exact tactic: to downplay the seriousness of the matter and to accentuate the discomfort in the room. Yet, who am I to decide these things? Clearly not the PSD.

Only minutes before, I have been to their floor - with additional security access where I was let in without query by a group from the lift - to find the DC. The thermostat is broken, she told me, reinforced by the Detective Sergeant. *My arse*, remains my loudest thought.

It is all pleasantries - *we are your friends* - with a slight holding back as they treat me like a suspect. I quietly weigh and measure them: she will be my friendly aggressor, he will be my silent comrade. My union rep, sits silently. The tapes go on after some fumbling with the wrappers - a disarming technique I have used many times and am not fooled by. The first forty minutes is me, reading the prepared statement and we reach a natural break as the tape ends.

- 210 -

After my two cigarettes the tapes are back, the temperature is hot and I am sweating. We circle around and the tap dance goes on until the tape finishes. The heat and lack of sleep have made me irritable. At the start of tape three I recap this, then ask my own questions: *where in the policy does it say this and that?* I get no answers, because there are none, then we go through the manipulation of figures and the topics of reform, promotion and self-interest. *Is that in the public interest? Should a serving police officer say that? Should a serving officer tell the public the truth? What would happen if all officers stood up to raise these issues?* I try to break it down, what would happen, hypothetically? And, If all officers raised the same issues what would that say about the service? He accuses me of twisting his words. I smile and give a final reply - having purposefully asked him to repeat his question. "You are basically asking a how long is a piece of string question."

The interview concludes and I ask again for my tapes, having asked for a copy up front. I get the same reply. *We don't give copies.* I ask again. *We don't give copies unless it goes to a hearing, but I'll ask.*

Exhausted I email the legals.

Thoughts turn to home and after a brief pit-stop I am on my way. In the back of my mind the earlier discussion with the Chief Inspector - explaining I would be seeing my doctor in the morning and may be off for a few weeks by way of the stress of the investigation. The train rumbles into the night and the knot in my stomach begins to unravel.

30th January:

The doctor signs me off for an initial two weeks. I have reached the end of even my capacity to deal with accumulated stress.

The relief on leaving the surgery washes over me almost immediately.

Briefly, I email my carrot-chopping 'welfare' sergeant, outlining the events which have resulted in my being signed off and all of a sudden he's attentive. Anything he can do to help. He even asks if I want to be referred to OH.

I'll think on it, knowing nothing internal is confidential.

8th of February:

The days have blurred into one since I last wrote, having slept and slept.

The situation presses down on me no less but the immediate, vomit-inducing physical effects have begun to subside and I am finding a new order. I haven't spoken to anyone outside of my home for a few days and, the more I withdraw, the harder it has been for me to step back in again and join any conversation. Today I did it for the first time and it didn't feel as bad as I had thought. I just hope my friends understand the depth of the damage done to me.

Seeing the local priest last Sunday was a relief and he left me with reading to do - not the Bible but C.S. Lewis. The first counselling session has started to help too. I have several channels now, getting everything out before it eats me alive. It had almost become a race.

There has been no news, not to my knowledge at least, from PSD. *Is it appropriate for a serving police officer to tell the public the truth?* Truly, that will stay with me forever - it may even be the final, rusty nail in the coffin I've built for everything I once put faith in. And, when I say everything, I do mean everything: the police, the commissions, the union. As the old saying goes, you should never put your eggs in one basket and I don't think I can be accused of it. If anything I am a man who has exhausted most of the baskets which exist.

The one thing to report on the work front is the Sergeant and the DI wanted to come and do a home visit. I don't know how they took it, or what was said when I replied that I would meet them at a train station as no representative of the GLP was welcome in my home.

It took a couple of days for a reply to come though and, if I said it was a surprise, I would be the proud wearer of flaming pants. They are waiting for the next update as to whether I will stay off or not. I think I will - I'm not ready and I've only just started down the road to feeling better after everything, but it is ultimately down to my GP - so they can pursue the home visit, in line with the brand new, unit specific, Attendance Management Policy. This raised a real belly laugh from me and deep concern in my wife, both for the same reason. I email back, asking for a copy of this policy and asking when it was introduced.

The reply elicits the expected response: they brought it in on the 31st of January, the day after I was signed off.

10th of February:

Sunday morning, the kids are having breakfast.

That's when, with my little girl on my lap, dusting me with crumbs, I get the message with a link to the Sunday paper. It's an article about the new police chief's guidelines on the use of social media by officers. It's a real gem: police officers should only discuss issues in private. I said this was all about control and good grief have they proved it. They used a clever tactic, making it look like all police officers who discuss the job - highlighting the negative - should be immediately thought of as drunk, mad, or doers of unspeakable evil. This is purely a set approach to belittle anyone who dares speak out. They have actually thrown transparency and public accountability - two of their favourite things to spout - out of the window and, worse still, they are forcing a sub-culture to exist in secret.

Corruption breeds behind closed doors, within circles. They have learned nothing but how to preserve themselves.

I see my name, mentioned quite incorrectly as being in trouble for social media, which actually makes me think back to a message I had about the Police College bringing my name up in respect of some social media conference. My QC is quoted saying the chiefs are using a sledgehammer to crack a nut. This makes me chuckle: I'm sure they would be delighted if they could say I was a raving loon. I've actually been waiting for them to say this - I live in constant preparation for being underwhelmed by the underhanded.

My batteries are recharging.

13th of February:

The GP has signed me off now, until the 4th of March. I need the time to be honest but I am feeling better, no matter what the PSD or the brothers try, with their investigations or attendance management policy. In the wider world, the Home Secretary has announced police integrity is a real issue.

After everything, I am now sure nothing will ever be fixed. The fear of starting policing all over again is too great. I have also realised I don't care about what decision the GLP come to about my job, not after all of this sorry shit shower. When I started out

I thought it was about being a good copper. As I come to the end of it, of this bit of it in any case, I know it was never about being a good copper: it was about trying to be a good person. A better one.

What I've learned about human nature, when people learn to ignore the little voice which sits whispering above the general sense of right and wrong, is they become corrupted. Vengeful, spiteful and self-preserving. When this becomes a culture, you are staring into the black, cancer-filled cage.

I don't know what this has achieved but something I do know, as certainly as I know it is a full moon when I see one of *those* smiles, is that however this ends I tried. I tried with everything I had and - though I may never be treated as a witness at the public inquiry I believe is so very dearly needed - no matter what comes next: I can look myself in the mirror, uniform or not.

18th of April:

It has been a while since I last sat down to write any journal entries.

Just look at the last few months: by ineptitude a woman was allowed to kill;

through corruption to manipulate figures, rape victims were told to retract allegations or otherwise poorly dealt with; a police officer is suing a garage for tripping over a kerb; whistleblowers are being arrested for talking to journalists. The union ballot on industrial rights went awry, with a low turn-out but a majority in favour. The central committees dismissed it. The end result is the long brewing civil war boiled over. They will now eat themselves, and it will be their own interests at the centre of whatever comes from it. Rural forces are merging units, reducing the number of traffic officers and also condensing the dog units across three counties - with no cover between four am and seven am. This was and always has been inevitable. The pile of cherries is collapsing and the majority of coppers appear to be only interested in the salary at the end of the month, none of the rest of it. Hence the boat remains largely unrocked. Most are rightly scared of being punished for saying anything at all.

Everything I have said is true and, scarier still, police whistleblowers are not needed if we are to follow the official lines of scorn and discouragement.

For my own part, I remain restricted and the PSD are dragging their heels. The latest update, two days ago, was that they have done 'some more work' on the file and are now sitting on it. I remain in limbo. A few months ago I wouldn't have taken this so well, while I was coming to terms with the futility of dependency on others. Now it doesn't matter.

I'd like to be able to finish this without it being left open-ended. With some final, conclusive, profound words but I don't know what the future will bring. Besides, the warm sunshine of spring is beaming down and the world looks better already. It's the ideal weather for picking a fight.

AFFLICTION

Affliction:

(Encyclopedia of Astrology)

Loosely applied to: (a) any inharmonious aspect to a planet, or (b) to any aspect, particularly the conjunction, parallel, square or opposition, to a malefic planet. Also by some authorities applied to a mundane or zodiacal parallel with, or when, besieged by both Infortunes (q.v.).

Some authorities consider that the sensitive degree on any House cusp can be afflicted, though any such consideration must be confined to instances where the birth-moment is known to a certainty. Unfavorably aspected.

***

Rafters creak gently under the weight of rope, a lulling sound in the otherwise silent bar. A gentle song of hardwood in the night, as moonlight falls through the ancient sash windows, thin glass covered in the quotations of Hemingway, Twain, Wilde and Kerouac. Casting their shadows in the strange swirls of handwriting projected large.

Maybe that's what life is, a blink of the eye and winking stars, the moon whispers, speculating with its soft caress.

The large mirrors behind the spirit shelves glisten too, twinkling in a bath of silver, reflecting Shakespeare into the quiet. *Fair is foul, and foul is fair,* whispers the furthest mirror left, closest to the timber framed structure of the old side, with its central pillar of oak rough-carved with the initials T.M. and the year 1702.

The shuffling from that open portal deafens as old ghosts glide across the flagstones, once covered in threadbare remnants of carpet and freed once again only months before. Cleaned and polished with love and hope, by the same hands now busy upon the rope, securing a heavy knot. Rough fibres prickle silvery skin in the shadows and the preparations are made. One last fall and the nocturnal sleep closes the door on the darkness of day. There is no clock to strike, so the soft breeze from the chimney suffices as the last of the coals glow and fade.

A shuffling of suit trouser and the soft clomp of a solid heel on the bar leave only the creaks of timber and rope to contemplate the beauty of the night.

***

Hampshire in the early nineteen-eighties was a hopeful place. Full of wonder, soft golden sunsets, hay bales, and trips to the old White Hart near Netley Marsh. It was a shame to have been dragged away, though on reflection he wasn't sure it would have made much difference in the grander scheme of things. The memory was held for reasons no more magical than the reminder of youth. Innocence of thought and deed. The permanent reminiscence of carefree days, when a world's boundary ended at the turning into Green Close, by the garages. Days long since gone now, despite him being far from old. Only just entering middle age, in truth.

The New Forest had given way to the rolling hills at the foot of the Chevin. The last stretch of what hikers call the Snakes' Back, where the Penine trail falls away into Milford and Duffield. The last rattle of a tail dotted with the left-overs of war. Anti-aircraft gun posts at the top of Firestone Quarry overlooking the Amber Valley as it reaches out towards Derby's farthest suburbs. The deep colours of the old sandstone excavations had always comforted him somewhat, a reminder of southerly sun over the water, out toward the needles from Milford-On-Sea. Further afield, Alport Stone, which became his place of peace. A finger of solid rock protruding from the basin of stone, stolen by men of old. A five county view on good days bewildering to the eye. It was here the scars had started to be carved into him. A crippling introvercy and fear of failure arising from little more than the childhood knocks which all but the most sensitive survive with ease. Despite his comfort in the far away secluded spots, close to the Hazelwood home on the row of houses known as Primrose Cottages, the village of Duffield itself would always be a graveyard to him. Pieces of himself buried in embarassment, frustration, and more physical pain. The wounds inflicted there would never truly heal, raw cuts periodically infected and inflamed by loss and love, leaving him bedridden as the years drew on.

London came and went, the agony of it excruciating as life gnawed at his bones. Rats from the darkest depths of the capital's sewers gnashing until it became to much for his tortured soul to bear and he surrendered to the wilds of the East. The bitter winters of East Anglia, a flattened scrubland on the

North Sea where only the sunrises made sense of his world, glistening on the still waters of Brightlingsea, overlooking St Osyth and Mersea Island. He dulled his anguish with alcohol, searing away at his body with a punishing nightly routine, until each evening he would collapse stuperous and numb. Each day came the blistering awakening, white hot burns from the return of everything at once flayed him. One way or another, death would find him. Hunt him out as he chased its overdue arrival. And so the old pub made sense.

***

The common misunderstanding of death, in particular when it is discussed or contemplated by mortal men and women, is incorrect. The reaper visits not when requested, nor absences itself when asked to stay away. The answer lies simply in the vast array of stars. Night diamonds glimmering in the darkness of sun's rest while the moon rules the hearts and minds of Earth. Such lessons are the lesser known lore by which the world holds its grant of existence.

The creaking rope, weighted by a man, was too much for the elderly rafter to carry and the groaning of the wood ceased its gentle song, screaming into the night as it wrenched itself apart, dry fibres tearing one by one until the chasm between them opened fully and the rope fell through. A sack-cloth thud on the floor, murmurs, then silence followed, while the moon played its music in light.

It seems to me that yet we sleep, we dream, whispered the mirrors to the man who continued to live.

J.J.P. 2006-2018

Cynefin ROAD

From Forever Completely

When the laughter subsided she placed her gentle hand on my arm. 'You know why we picked you, don't you?'

'I'll take this!' the Goat leapt in. 'You were always a naughty, impetuous, disobedient little so and so. You never followed orders properly, even in the old wars. You'd just gallivant around doing the right thing with a smile on your face but always in your own hodgepodge way.' He eyed me, for once not boggling — measuring me to make sure I'd connected this to the almost inexplicable approach I'd taken to magick. I understood it. They'd needed my traits as they'd said.

'So that's why we forced you to go back for this,' she squeezed my arm a little. It was tender and apologetic but not in the way it meant sorry. 'You needed to be a new person too, because it's where the silver had to grow from so you could close the door. But you also needed to be taught a lesson for your past behaviour.'

'What's that word you use? Ah, yes, temerity,' the Goat chipped in. 'You had to be punished for your temerity and acts of insubordination, so we made sure your life wasn't an easy ride.'

'I got what I deserved,' I said. 'I wasn't surprised, flabbergasted, nor upset. It made sense and I laughed harder...

CPSIA information can be obtained
at www.ICGtesting.com
Printed in the USA
BVHW08s1924010818
523277BV00011B/782/P